PAPER CHASE

PAPER CHASE

by
Bob Cook

St. Martin's Press
New York

PAPER CHASE. Copyright © 1989 by Bob Cook. All rights reserved. Printed in the United States of America. No part of this book may be used or reproduced in any manner whatsoever without written permission except in the case of brief quotations embodied in critical articles or reviews. For information, address St. Martin's Press, 175 Fifth Avenue, New York, N.Y. 10010.

Cook, Bob.
      Paper chase / Bob Cook.
         p.   cm.
      ISBN 0-312-04400-3
      I. Title.
    PR6053.05183P37   1990
    823'.914—dc20   89-77957
                                                   CIP

First pubished in Great Britain by Victor Gollancz Ltd.

First U.S. Edition
10 9 8 7 6 5 4 3 2 1

ONE

Clive Ogden locked up his car and swore. He had forgotten to bring his overcoat, and the wind was sharp and unforgiving. It sliced through his clothes and made his limbs quiver with cold. A younger man might have shrugged it off, but Ogden was nearly seventy and this kind of weather played havoc with his bones.

"Oh well," he muttered. "Nothing for it, I suppose."

He turned up his collar, popped a stick of bubble-gum into his mouth, and went through the gates of the cemetery. There were few people around, and he had little trouble in finding the place he wanted.

Ogden was a lean, gangly man, over six feet four inches tall, who walked in long, loping strides. He was totally bald, save for a few wisps of grey at the back and sides, and his face was adorned by a permanent yellow grin. These features conspired to make him look like a benevolent old skeleton, escaped from some museum of natural history.

Up ahead, he could see three men standing around a freshly-filled grave. He recognised their faces: they were all contemporaries who had worked with Ogden in MI5, the British security service. Every so often, they would meet at the funeral of some colleague, chat about old times, exchange gossip, and go home. At the time of their retirement, there had been fifteen of these friends. Now, apart from Ogden, there were only three.

One was a massive, red-faced man with thick white sideboards and a foul-smelling meerschaum pipe. His name was Fergus Buchanan which had caused much confusion over the years, since he was not remotely Scottish. Despite Buchanan's irritated denials, his colleagues had always insisted that he was really an absentee Highland landlord, and they had dubbed him the Laird.

Beside him stood an elegant, well-groomed man called Jeremy Beauchamp who wore tailored suits and a luxuriant chestnut-brown hairpiece. There was much speculation about what, if

5

anything, the toupee concealed, but nobody had ever dared to ask. Beauchamp's Olympian dignity ruled out any such inquiries.

The third man was frail and small, and leaned on a walking stick. His name was Godfrey Croft, but he was known as the Vicar. He was not, of course, a man of the cloth: he had earned the soubriquet forty years earlier when his eager, rubicund features lent him the appearance of a jolly young clergyman. Now he looked more like a retired bishop: two watery eyes peered out from a brown old scrotum of a face, and his scalp was speckled with liver spots. But to his former colleagues, he was still the Vicar.

"Afternoon, chaps," Ogden said briskly, as he arrived at the graveside. "Show's over, I see. The bloody traffic held me up."

"Not to worry, Clive," the Vicar replied. "You didn't miss much. We were the only ones who showed."

"Really?" Ogden blinked. "Just the four of us?"

"Afraid so. Jumbo had no relations, apparently. At least, no close ones."

"In that case," Ogden said, "who's that chap?"

"Who?"

Ogden pointed to someone standing about twenty feet away. He was a youngish man with a grimy raincoat and a cigarette in his hand.

"That fellow there," Ogden said. "The grey eminence."

"No idea," said the Laird. "He didn't join us for the service. Just lurked in the background, like he's doing now."

"Some kind of voyeur," Beauchamp suggested. "You get the oddest people in cemeteries."

"Never mind," Ogden said. "How was the service?"

"Pretty half-hearted. The padre kept glancing at his watch."

Ogden shook his head and looked down at the grave.

"Poor old Jumbo," he sighed. "I only heard about it yesterday."

"Stroke, apparently," the Vicar said. "The hospital found our names in his address book. There was nobody else to notify."

"Didn't Jumbo ever have a wife?" Beauchamp asked.

"Wife?" the Laird chuckled. "Wife? You're joking, of course. Jumbo had no use for women. I always said he was—"

'Oh, really," Beauchamp groaned. "Just because a man's

unmarried, it doesn't *automatically* follow that he's one of the brown-hat brigade."

"Quite right," Ogden nodded. "After all, only two of us still have wives: Jeremy and the Vicar."

"One," Beauchamp corrected him. "My old girl died last year."

"Sorry to hear it, Jeremy," Ogden sympathised. "It's a few years since mine passed on, but I remember it took me a while to bounce back. She went peacefully, I hope?"

"Dicky ticker," Beauchamp shrugged. "No pain."

"Anyway," said the Laird, "we all *were* married, which is more than could be said for Jumbo Wagstaffe."

"Doesn't prove he was a nancy."

"There were other pointers," the Laird insisted. "Do you remember that chap he shared digs with? A painter or something—"

"He was a sculptor."

"That's the fellow," the Laird agreed. "Now *he* was definitely a pillow-chewer, and I always maintained—"

"Jumbo was positively vetted on at least six occasions," Ogden reminded him. "And that kind of thing usually comes out in the wash."

"Does it?" said the Laird pointedly. "If you say so, Clive."

"Well, who cares if he was a you-know-what?" said the Vicar. "He was a decent enough chap. One of the best medium-pace bowlers we ever had. I remember that match we played against Naval Intelligence in '49—or was it '48? Anyway, Jumbo took three for eighteen. None of your lower-order rubbish, either. Those were all prime wickets."

"I don't care if he was a second Larwood," the Laird insisted. "The man was still an arse-bandit."

He rapped his pipe emphatically against the heel of his shoe, releasing a shower of thick ash.

"It's a bit disrespectful," Ogden said, gazing thoughtfully at the grave.

"What is?"

"Speculating about Jumbo's proclivities by his graveside."

"Quite right," Beauchamp nodded. "Let's change the subject."

"That's not what I meant," Ogden said. "I just feel it would be more appropriate to continue this conversation in a pub."

7

"Good idea," the Laird grinned.

"It's Jumbo I'm thinking of," Ogden added hastily.

"Oh, naturally," the Vicar said. "And besides, it's raining."

"That settles it," Beauchamp decided. "There's one over the road. Follow me."

They tramped over to a dusty little public house and found nothing there except for one bored landlord, two silent darts-players, and a juke-box which played something by Nat King Cole.

"Suddenly the rain seems very attractive," Beauchamp muttered.

"Not to worry," Ogden said, and he ordered a round of drinks. The friends took a table by the window.

"I think I preferred the cemetery," the Vicar said as he glanced around him. "There was more life in it."

The Laird scowled at his glass.

"They share the same proprietor," he decided. "This gin tastes like embalming fluid."

"Something wrong?" inquired the landlord.

"Not at all," Ogden said soothingly. "My friend was just praising your gin. It brings the colour back to one's cheeks."

The landlord grunted, and returned to his daydream.

"It's a bit silly, really," Beauchamp said.

"What is?"

"We only ever run into each other at funerals. Never anywhere else."

"You're right," Ogden said. "We should meet more often."

"No reason not to," said the Vicar. "We all live in London, or near it. And I don't know about you chaps, but my diary isn't exactly overflowing."

"That settles it," the Laird said, as he filled his pipe. "We'll organise a get-together."

"Come to my place," the Vicar suggested. "I'm not as mobile as I was, thanks to my hip replacement. And my wife won't mind. Well, not much."

"The delectable Sybil," Ogden grinned. 'How is the old girl?"

"Oh, fine, fine," said the Vicar, with a touch of regret.

Ogden blew a large pink bubble of gum, which took his colleagues by surprise.

"What the devil's that?" the Laird asked.

"Never seen bubble-gum before?"

"Not in your mouth."

"I finally gave up smoking," Ogden explained. "Tried chewing-gum to take my mind off it. It didn't really work. This stuff's much better."

"Hello, hello," Beauchamp said. "It's the chap from the cemetery."

"The grey eminence," Ogden said.

The man in the raincoat bought himself a drink, and came over to their table. In most respects, he was just as nondescript as when seen from a distance: his clothes, haircut and expression were bland and uninformative. But his eyes were bleak and sardonic—like a professional torturer's, Ogden thought—and if the man had any charm he kept it well hidden.

"Afternoon," he said. "Mind if I join you?"

The others glanced at each other inquiringly.

"Not in the least," Ogden said. "Pint of bitter for me."

The man shook his head and sat down.

"You don't want another pint," he said curtly.

"Don't I?" Ogden blinked.

"You're driving, Mr Ogden. I wouldn't want you to get into trouble. That's why I'm here: to stop you and your friends from getting into trouble."

If his remarks were intended to surprise his audience, they were entirely successful. After a pause, Ogden said, "How do you know my name?"

"I know all your names," the man said.

He pointed to the Vicar and said, "Godfrey Croft. Age seventy-two. Served 1944 to 1979. Directorate 'A'."

"Guilty, my Lord," the Vicar replied.

"Fergus Buchanan," the man went on. "Age sixty-six. Served 1951 to 1980. Directorate 'K'."

He took a sip of his orange juice.

"Next there's Mr Jeremy Beauchamp," he said. "Age sixty-eight. Served 1946 to 1977 in Directorates 'C' and 'F', then left us to run an antique business. Currently retired."

"Gosh," Ogden said. "You haven't chucked in the junk shop, have you Jeremy?"

"Two years ago," Beauchamp nodded. "It never made any money. I couldn't bear to sell the best pieces, you see . . ."

9

"All those Chinese vases," the Vicar mused. "I remember you were very keen on that Oriental stuff."

"Lastly," the man said, "we have Mr Clive Ogden. Age seventy. Served in Directorate 'K' from 1944 to 1961. Transferred to SIS, and stayed there until 1970 when he returned to our lot until retirement in 1981."

"I was homesick," Ogden chuckled. "Anyway, dear boy, isn't it time you introduced yourself? I take it you're from MI5?"

"My name's Geoff Stringer. I'm with 'B' Directorate. And it's not called MI5 any more."

"I know, I know," Ogden sighed. "'The Security Service', isn't it? I always thought MI5 was more romantic. My wife thought so too. What can we do for you, Mr Stringer?"

"Is it about the cricket match?" the Vicar asked hopefully.

"The what?"

"The cricket match. You know, the inter-service championship. MI5 versus MI6, Signals, and Naval Intelligence."

"There's no such thing," Stringer said.

"You mean they've stopped it? Good Lord. But it was an annual fixture . . . Don't you play cricket, Mr Stringer?"

Stringer took a deep breath.

"No," he said patiently. "Football's my game."

"Well that's not too bad, I suppose," Beauchamp said. "I don't mind a spot of rugger myself . . ."

"No," Stringer said. "Football. The one with the round ball."

The Vicar's jaw dropped in horror.

"Good heavens," he breathed. "Are you saying MI5 are playing . . . football?"

Stringer's eyes rolled upwards.

"No," he said heavily. "The Security Service doesn't play football. It doesn't play any games. It just gets on with the business of protecting national security. Now, if you don't mind—"

"But you just said—"

"I said *I* played it," Stringer barked.

"Oh. I see."

The Vicar scratched his jaw in contemplation.

"So they've cancelled the cricket matches. What a damned shame."

10

"Fuck the cricket matches," Stringer snarled. "Just listen to what I have to say, will you?"

The old men looked at each other in surprise. Then the Laird tugged an imaginary forelock and said, "Yes, master. Oi be listening closely, master."

"We're all ears," Beauchamp said.

"Anything you say, Mr Swinger," Ogden grinned, and he blew another pink gum-bubble.

"The name's Stringer, and I'm here to give you characters an official warning. You know there's been a lot of hassle recently about former members of the security services writing unauthorised memoirs and talking to the Press about their careers. Well, we're having a crack-down. Everybody is getting a verbal caution as well as a written one from the Director-General."

"Not me, Slinger," Ogden said. "Nothing from the D-G in my letter-box."

"It's *Stringer*," Stringer said irritably, "and the letters haven't gone out yet. But get this straight: if any of you is stupid enough to think he can earn a few extra quid by telling his life-story to the newspapers, he'll go straight to gaol."

"Do not pass 'go', do not collect two hundred pounds," the Vicar said.

"Exactly," Stringer nodded. "So the message is: keep your traps shut. Your careers are state secrets, understand? Anything you say to anybody—however trivial the information—will land you in the slammer."

"Don't worry, Mr Springer," Ogden said gently. "None of us had plans of that sort—"

"Don't change your minds," Stringer said. "There'll be hell to pay if you do."

He finished his drink and got up.

"Now," he said, "if that's understood, I'll be on my way."

"Off to see other colleagues?" Beauchamp inquired.

"Yeah."

"In that case," the Laird said, "can I offer you a tip?"

Stringer frowned.

"What is it?"

"You could try to be more polite with the others. You know, a few 'pleases' and 'thank yous'."

"It wouldn't hurt," Beauchamp agreed.

11

"Bollocks," Stringer snorted. "Just do as you're told, okay?"

He walked out of the pub, leaving the old men shaking their heads in disbelief.

"What a rude man," Beauchamp said.

"Incredible," Ogden agreed. "Which slum did they pluck him out of?"

"A footballer," the Vicar said bitterly, as if that explained everything.

The Laird chewed his pipe irritably.

"There was a time," he said, "when fellows like that weren't allowed anywhere near MI5."

"You know," Ogden said, "I've a good mind to complain to the D-G. After forty years of service, I don't expect to be treated like a bloody criminal."

"Damned insulting," Beauchamp agreed. "Things have obviously changed for the worse in the old firm."

"They certainly have," said the Vicar. "Fancy abolishing the inter-service cricket match. It's—it's downright vandalism."

"In that case," Ogden said, "I think we should consider our response."

"Definitely," the Laird said.

"A formal complaint," Beauchamp said.

"Absolutely."

"Death to footballers," cried the Vicar.

TWO

"Three pounds," said the taxi driver as he pulled up outside the hotel.

His passenger yawned, paid the fare, and got out of the car. The Hotel Leftera seemed much like any other low-budget accommodation on Cyprus: peeling, fly-blown and shabby. But the man was not particularly bothered. In the last three days he had slept for a total of five hours, and under those circumstances the whole world looked somewhat frayed at the edges. And besides, the man had not come to Larnaca for a holiday.

He picked up his travelling-bag and introduced himself to Mr Leftera, the owner.

"I phoned from the airport," the man said. "Name of Carter."

Mr Leftera nodded and took a key off the wall.

"This way."

Carter followed him up a gloomy stairway and into a small, grimy bedroom. There was not much light: the cracked window-pane had last been cleaned in about 1908, and the electric bulb just made the room seem darker. But Carter could make out a ramshackle bed with a sagging mattress, a coat-rack, a small table, and a chair with one leg missing.

"Okay?" Mr Leftera inquired.

"It'll do," Carter said.

"Three pounds a night."

Carter paid for two nights and took the key.

"How do I get to the harbour?" he asked.

Mr Leftera pointed towards the window, which didn't mean much.

"We are next to St Lazarus Square, okay?"

Carter nodded.

"You go three blocks that way," Mr Leftera said. "Find Athens Avenue. That runs along the waterfront. It's all there."

"Thanks," Carter said.

Mr Leftera went downstairs, and Carter threw himself down

onto the bed. Just half an hour, he decided, and then I'll go out. Just half an hour. Seconds later, he was fast asleep.

It may have been half an hour later when he awoke, it may have been longer. The door creaked open and shut, and Carter looked up to see a man leaning over his bed. He was a large man, barrel-chested, with grey hair cut very short and a disconcerting stare. It took a couple of seconds for Carter to remember who he was.

"Kyle," he said. "What are you doing here?"

The man did not offer an immediate reply. He continued to stare down at Carter, as if trying to make up his mind about something. Then, in a low murmur, he said, "The Lord abhors bloodthirsty and deceitful men."

"What was that?" Carter blinked. "How did you know I was here?"

Kyle looked around the room until he came across Carter's door key. He then returned to the door, locked it, and put the key in his pocket.

"What's going on, Kyle?"

Kyle continued to ignore Carter, and picked up Carter's bag. He threw the contents onto the floor, knelt down, and began to sift through them.

"For Christ's sake," Carter said irritably. "Will you stop playing silly buggers and tell me what you're doing?"

Kyle smiled grimly as he inspected Carter's papers.

"His mouth is filled with cursing and deceit and oppression," he muttered. "Under his tongue are mischief and iniquity."

Carter shook his head in confusion.

"I think I'm still dreaming," he said. "Kyle, have you got a new job with the Cyprus police? Because if you haven't, kindly stop going through my belongings."

Kyle put down the paper he was reading, stood up, and walked over to Carter's bed. Then, without any hesitation, he hit Carter full in the face.

"The talk of a fool is a rod for his back," Kyle explained, and he went back to Carter's possessions.

Carter sat up and clutched his face.

"Oh, God," he moaned. "You mad bastard, you've broken my fucking nose. What's the matter with you, Kyle? I've done nothing to you."

Kyle glanced at him sharply.

"A truthful witness saves lives," he declared, "but one who utters lies is a betrayer."

"Betrayer?" Carter said. "What do you mean? How have I betrayed you?"

Kyle grunted, and continued to look through Carter's papers, while their owner tried to stanch the blood pouring from his nose. If Kyle was looking for anything specific, he did not find it. Finally, he stood up and returned to the bedside.

"I shall punish thee according to the fruit of thy doings, sayeth the Lord," Kyle declared.

"Punish me?" Carter said. "What on earth for? I haven't done a thing. I honestly don't know why—"

"Who that was innocent ever perished?" Kyle interrupted.

"Please Kyle, will you drop all this biblical gibberish and tell me what you want? I've told you I was sorry about the order. It wasn't my fault, and you know it. As a matter of fact, that's why I'm here. I heard a rumour that the *Flavio*'s in Larnaca. If you come with me to the harbour, we might be able to . . ."

Carter did not bother to finish the sentence. Kyle was not listening, and he clearly was not interested in any proposition Carter might put to him.

"And all the people among whom thou art shall see the work of the Lord," Kyle said bitterly, "for it is a terrible thing that I will do with thee."

Carter began to edge away from the bed. One glance at Kyle's red face and bulging eyeballs made it plain that Kyle was beyond any form of rational persuasion.

"I'm calling the manager," Carter said. "This is getting—"

Kyle leaped onto Carter and pinned him to the bed. Then he clamped one beefy hand across Carter's face, and wound his other arm around the back of Carter's head. Kyle took a deep breath, and jerked his elbows apart. With a muffled crunch, Carter's neck broke.

Kyle got off the bed, and nodded in satisfaction.

"So perish all thine enemies, O Lord," he declared.

THREE

"That does it," Ogden declared. "I'm definitely complaining."

"Me too," the Laird said. "It's totally unacceptable."

"Why," Beauchamp said, "he's almost as bad as that man Stringer."

"Quite unprovoked, too," said the Vicar.

The cautionary letter from the D-G had finally arrived. It was headed, "Dear Pensioner", and was brusque to the point of rudeness. Ogden & Co. were told that under no circumstances could they reveal any information about their careers. Failure to heed the warning would result in loss of pension, prosecution, and imprisonment. The letter was signed "P. Lazenby, Director-General".

"How shall we play this?" Ogden asked. "Complain by letter, or demand to see the chap and let him have it verbally?"

"Oh, verbally," Beauchamp said.

"With both barrels," the Laird said.

"I think you're being quite ridiculous about this. Why don't you just shut up and do as the man asks?"

The dissenting voice belonged to the Vicar's wife, Sybil. She was a sturdy, angular lady, who spent much of her life disapproving of things. She disapproved of frivolity, facetiousness, and insubordination. Her husband's friends were guilty of all three, so she disapproved of them too.

"The D-G's quite right, of course," she said. "You're obliged to keep totally silent about your careers. I really don't see what all the fuss is about."

"The fuss," Ogden said, "is about the way they're treating us. You should have heard that chap Springer: a nasty, foul-mouthed street urchin, with the manners of a Cossack. It was quite uncalled for."

"So's this letter," the Laird added, jabbing his pipe-stem at the offending missive. "All these crude threats, as if we were a bunch of convicts on probation. We had no intention of writing our memoirs, or talking to the Press. Why should we?"

"The D-G isn't to know that," Sybil said. "And you shouldn't take it so personally. It's a stereotyped letter, and it's worded to cover all categories of Pensioner."

"Things have obviously gone downhill since we left," the Vicar sighed. "Did I tell you, Sybil, they've abolished the inter-service cricket matches?"

"You've told me about twenty times, Godfrey."

"Oh," the Vicar grunted. "Well it's not good enough, that's all."

"You silly men," Sybil chided, "can't you see, it's become another world? They employ specialists. Trained people. Not your sort, at all. I know it's sad, but—but I suppose it's progress, isn't it?"

"Specialists," the Laird said witheringly.

"Trained people," Beauchamp spat.

"Ruffians, you mean," the Vicar said. "Louts like Stringer. What's he trained in, eh? What's his speciality?"

"He's got an honours degree in hooliganism," Ogden said. "But look, chaps, Slinger may just be an aberration. I've been thinking about what Sybil's been saying, and she's right: the old firm is much too big for the D-G to write to all retired staff—"

"Exactly," Sybil said.

"—and I suspect he didn't write this wretched letter. Some dimwitted secretary did it for him."

"Of course," Sybil nodded.

"So," Ogden went on, "the D-G probably hasn't even read what's been sent out in his name. The chances are he'd be incensed if anyone told him."

"That's a point," Beauchamp said.

"In fact," Ogden concluded, "I bet the D-G's a thoroughly decent chap who'd put a stop to this nonsense if anyone complained. So let's complain."

"Oh really," Sybil snorted. "For a moment, I thought you were going to be sensible about this."

"But I am," Ogden insisted. "They might be letting in riff-raff like Swinger at the lowest ranks, but I'm sure the D-G's still the right kind of fellow. Let's see him."

★

And so, despite Sybil's misgivings, Ogden and his friends fixed an appointment to see the Director-General at MI5 headquarters in Curzon Street. As they were shown into his office, they were somewhat surprised to see that the D-G wore a brown suit. They were even more surprised to see Geoff Stringer sitting by the D-G's desk.

"Good morning," the D-G said. "I understand you want to lodge a formal complaint about something."

"That's right," Ogden said. "But I think it would be best if Mr Slinger wasn't present. You see, the complaint partially concerns him."

"Thought it might," the D-G nodded. "That's why I've asked Mr Stringer to join us."

"Indeed," Ogden blinked. "Oh well, if that's how you do things around here, so be it. To begin with, we want to complain about Springer's approach to us the other day."

"What was wrong with it?" Stringer asked.

"Pretty tactless choice of venue, wasn't it?" the Laird said. "A colleague's funeral. Couldn't you have found a better opportunity?"

"No," Stringer said. "It meant I could get four of you in one hit. Saved me a lot of travelling, didn't it?"

"I suppose it did," Beauchamp said drily. "And that's all that matters, isn't it?"

"Then," Ogden continued, "there was Mr Swinger's tone. Without any provocation, he spoke to us in a rude and threatening manner."

"Crap," Stringer said briskly. "I was there to lay down the law. That's exactly what I did."

"There he goes again," the Vicar said indignantly. "It really won't do, you know."

The D-G's face remained expressionless.

"Anything else?" he asked.

"Yes," Ogden said. "This letter we've received. It was sent in your name—"

"Right," the D-G agreed. "I wrote it."

Ogden stared at him in disbelief.

"You wrote it," he repeated. "But—but . . ."

"Bit crude, wasn't it?" the Laird said. "Bit rough around the edges?"

"What's the matter?" Stringer said. "Is there a spelling mistake in there?"

"That's not what I meant. Don't you think it was impolite?"

The D-G exchanged glances with Stringer, and smiled.

"It wasn't meant to be rude," he said. "It was businesslike, that's all. We want you to know exactly where you stand."

"You could put the message across more delicately," Beauchamp said. "A spot of tact wouldn't hurt."

"Come on, gentlemen," the D-G said, "we're all grown men. There's no need to get worked up over a simple cautionary letter."

"In forty years here," Ogden said firmly, "I never once received a letter like that. With respect, none of your predecessors would have sent it out."

The D-G shrugged indifferently.

"I wouldn't know," he said.

"And what about the cricket?" the Vicar demanded.

"Eh?"

"The inter-service championship."

"What's that got to do with anything?"

"Well," said the Vicar, "Stringer says you've abolished it. I think it's a jolly bad sign. What's this outfit coming to when Pensioners are insulted and nobody plays cricket any more?'

"Hear, hear," said the Laird.

"Quite right," Beauchamp agreed.

The D-G took a deep breath, and slapped his hand down on the desk.

"That's enough," he decided. "I've heard all I'm going to. Now listen to me, you characters. You were given those warnings because some of your colleagues have been breaking their confidence. Too many people have been publishing memoirs, writing articles on Intelligence, and generally chattering to the Press. It's got to stop.

"Mr Stringer was perfectly entitled to speak to you when and where he did. It seems to me that your complaint about his manner is the same as your complaint about the cricket: things aren't matching up to your high social standards. Well, that's just too bad.

"And I'm not apologising for my own letter. I was making a point, and if you haven't understood it, I'll repeat it one more

19

time: don't discuss your careers with anyone. Don't talk to the Press, the publishers, or any other inquiring soul who comes knocking on your front doors. Ignore my warning, and you'll be in big trouble. Now, if you'll excuse me, I've got a lot of work to do. Good morning."

FOUR

"Well?" Sybil said. "What did you expect?"

The others said nothing, and continued to stare down at the Vicar's drawing-room carpet with hurt, indignant expressions.

"I did warn you," she added.

"You did indeed, Sybil," the Vicar murmured wearily.

"It's all changed," Sybil said, as she poured out more cups of tea. "It isn't the Athenaeum any more. And you'd better get used to the fact."

There was a clear note of satisfaction in her voice which Ogden found highly provocative.

"We were fully entitled to complain," he said irritably. "They've no right to send ill-mannered young yahoos out to harass—"

"They've every right," Sybil said. "They did it, didn't they? And with the D-G's full approval."

"He's another yobbo," Beauchamp said. "That was the real shock. Wears a brown suit, if you please. I mean, spivs like Stringer can creep into the best outfits. Can't be helped, I suppose. But fancy putting one of them in charge of the show. *In charge*, for heaven's sake!"

"Bloody disgrace," the Laird agreed, and he blew out a cloud of angry pipe-smoke.

"Such a distasteful man," said the Vicar. "You know, after all that, I'm sorely tempted to write my memoirs, just to spite the fellow."

"Hear, hear," Ogden said. "It never occurred to me to put pen to paper. But if the wretched people are going to make such a song and dance about it, I'm willing to think again."

Sybil puckered her lips.

"Childish," she observed.

"Trouble is," said the Laird, "what the devil have we got to write about? I don't know about you chaps, but my time in MI5

21

wasn't exactly brimful of excitement. Oh, there was a spot of occasional fun—"

"The cricket matches," nodded the Vicar.

"—but none of what the public wants: heavy-duty espionage intrigue, moles, microfilm, all that stuff. In fact, my career was so bloody dull I've forgotten most of it."

The others sighed in agreement.

"Our best times were during the war," Ogden said. "They taught us codes and ciphers and things, and showed us how to use guns. Pity I never had to use 'em. Anyway, after the war it all rather dried up. I expected a bit more excitement in MI6— that's why I transferred. But that turned out to be even more boring than MI5."

"Is that why you came back to us?" Beauchamp inquired.

"'Fraid so," Ogden admitted. "Oh, I did pick up one or two good tales along the way. But nothing to build an entire memoir on."

"What sort of tales?" the Vicar asked.

"The odd dirty trick here and there," Ogden shrugged. "A spot of illegal bugging. A couple of kidnappings."

The Laird waved his hand disdainfully.

"We all know stories like that," he said. "I know some pretty scandalous things about Northern Ireland. Nothing first-hand, though."

"In that case," the Vicar said brightly, "why don't we pool all our stories? Between us we might have enough for a memoir."

Sybil frowned sternly at her husband.

"Godfrey—" she began.

"Now that's an idea," Beauchamp said. "If we strung them all together . . ."

"You'll go to prison," Sybil said. "Are you men deaf as well as stupid? The D-G warned you—"

"To buggery with the D-G," the Laird declared. "We'll leave the country."

Sybil snorted.

"We aren't all as rich as you, Fergus Buchanan. Some of us have to live on our pensions—MI5 pensions, which will be cut off, no matter where we are."

"I'm not that bloody rich," the Laird grinned, "I need the pension too. But that's not the point. If the memoirs are good

22

enough, we'll be paid handsomely for them. No more need for crumbs from MI5's table, eh?"

"What a lovely idea," the Vicar sighed.

"It's an established formula," Beauchamp said. "We publish, the Government bans, the public buys, and we make a killing."

"Rubbish," Sybil insisted. "Absolute rot. Look, you silly men: MI5 memoirs are ten a penny. Your 'established formula' has been used so often that there's a glut on the market. People have had enough of old spy stories, and they don't want any more, unless they're really sensational, and yours jolly well aren't."

The others glanced at each other uncomfortably.

"So," Sybil concluded, "you don't stand to make any money. But you do stand to lose your pensions, and you might go to gaol."

Ogden absently twirled the hair in his ears.

"I'm afraid Sybil's right," he conceded. "Even if we could string a book together, the income from it would be piddling. I do know some good yarns—things that would still embarrass the Government—but they're still not good enough. Wrong league."

"That's the trouble with truth," the Laird observed. "It's too bloody boring."

"People want their truth to resemble fiction," Beauchamp said. "Lots of glamour, derring-do . . ."

"Violence," Ogden said.

"Sex," said the Vicar. "Must have sex."

"Exactly," Sybil said heavily. "And what can you give them, Godfrey? Cricket matches."

"Oh Lord," Ogden said weakly. "Em—what were we talking about?"

"Truth," Beauchamp said. "The problem therewith."

"Ah yes," Ogden said. "That is a headache—"

He stopped and screwed up his eyes in thought.

"Now wait a minute," he murmured. "Just wait a minute . . ."

He reached into his pocket and drew out a stick of bubble-gum. After a few chews, he leaned back in his armchair and put his hands behind his head.

"The trouble with truth," he repeated.

The others said nothing and watched curiously as a large green bubble formed below Ogden's nose. When it finally exploded, Ogden sat bolt upright and snapped his fingers.

23

"I've got it," he declared.

"Oh dear," Sybil groaned, as she saw the twinkle in Ogden's eyes. "What now?"

"Look," Ogden reasoned, "we can't print the truth, because that would put us in chokey. And nobody wants to read the truth anyway. So let's tell lies."

"What do you mean?" asked the Laird.

"Let's write fictitious memoirs. We'll say we were in Intelligence—which is perfectly true—but instead of telling boring true stories, let's tell a lot of sensational lies. Really spectacular whoppers. The public want exciting espionage yarns—let's give 'em some."

The Vicar's eyes bulged in shock.

"But—but you can't do that!"

"Why ever not?" Ogden inquired.

"The Government would just deny the stories," Beauchamp said.

"Let them," Ogden grinned. "Don't you see? Nobody would believe the buggers. Besides, official policy is neither to confirm nor deny anybody's memoirs. But they'll still have to ban the book—"

"Why?" asked the Laird. "If it's full of bullshit—"

"That wouldn't matter. It would still be the memoirs of a former employee of MI5, bound by a life-long duty of confidentiality. They'd have to ban it. But if the stories were good enough, the Americans would pay a fortune for them—"

"And the Australians," Beauchamp observed.

"Even the Russians," the Vicar chuckled. "What sport!"

"And they'd still gaol you," Sybil insisted.

"What on earth for?" Ogden grinned. "The only crime we'd commit would be to claim we once worked for MI5. Can you really see the Attorney-General taking a bunch of old coots like us to court just for saying that? Even this government wouldn't be that daft. They'd become a laughing-stock . . ."

"So what?" Sybil said. "They're already a laughing-stock. That won't save you."

"No, dear," said the Vicar, "I think Clive's right. The memoirs would be a work of fiction. And there are lots of examples of ex-Intelligence chaps writing spy novels. Le Carré, Graham Greene . . ."

"I see," Sybil nodded grimly. "And you can write equally well, can you?"

Ogden's eyes rolled upwards.

"Of course we can't, Sybil darling," he said patiently. "We don't need to. Their books purport to be fiction. Ours won't. Nobody expects non-fiction to be well written, do they?"

"Right," the Laird agreed. "We'd have the best of all worlds. Bloody clever idea, Clive."

Ogden grinned and exploded another gum-bubble.

"Thank you, dear boy. All in the day's work for us geniuses, you know. Now, what's this book going to look like?"

"Well, for starters," Beauchamp said, "it should just be the memoir of one man. We'll pool all our ideas, of course, but the book should have one nominal author. It'll look more authentic that way."

Since Beauchamp had worked in the antique business, his opinions on the subject of forgery were held to be authoritative. The others nodded in approval.

"That sounds reasonable," Ogden said. "Which of us will it be? How about you, Laird?"

"Yes," the Vicar agreed. "You were always the athletic type: muscle-bound, fearless—"

"Sod off," the Laird grinned. "I'm no James Bond."

"You've got a black belt in ju-jitsu," Ogden said accusingly.

"Acquired forty years ago," the Laird countered, "and it's at least twenty-five years since I made any use of it. End of argument."

"In that case," Ogden said, "why not Jeremy? 'The candid autobiography of an intrepid double-agent and antique dealer.'"

"Expert in everything from microdots to Ming vases," the Laird added.

"Dead-letter boxes and Delft pottery . . ."

"I don't think so, somehow," Beauchamp smiled. "But I'd say the Vicar was a prime candidate."

"Ah yes," Ogden said. "You're the boffin after all, Vicar. All your technological experience: radios, phone-taps, and so on."

"I suppose so . . ." the Vicar said hesitantly.

"Why, you were just one step away from exploding fountain pens and nuclear-powered Aston Martins," the Laird observed. "Can't be bad."

Sybil could contain herself no longer.

"Out of the question," she snapped. "I won't let Godfrey make a fool of himself."

"Oh, come on, Sybil," Ogden laughed. "Don't be such a party-pooper. I'm sure you'd enjoy being married to Godfrey Croft, Superspy."

"The intrepid Croft," Beauchamp said dramatically. "KGB agents trembled at his name. Beautiful women melted in his arms—"

"Over my dead body!" Sybil shouted. "Godfrey, I absolutely forbid it."

"Oh dear," said the Vicar. "I think Sybil means it, chaps."

"I most certainly do."

"In that case," said the Laird, "there's only one man left. Clive . . ."

Ogden blew another green balloon, and thought about it.

"You really think so?" he said.

"Definitely," said the Laird. "After all, you were in both branches of Intelligence."

Ogden nodded.

"True."

"And you're easily the most resourceful chap here."

"True, true."

"So why not?"

Ogden raised his hands in resignation.

"Why not indeed? Very well: Clive Ogden, Cold Warrior Extraordinaire. So be it."

"Good man," said the Vicar. "Now, how shall we do this?"

"There should be one writer," Beauchamp said, "to give the book a unified style. Anyone here ever written anything?"

"Not me," Ogden said.

"Ditto," said the Laird.

"I wrote a book once," the Vicar admitted.

"Did you really?" Ogden blinked. "What was it?"

"A history of the Test Match from 1900 to 1910. It was privately printed."

"I bet it was," Ogden smiled. "Still, that puts you one up on the rest of us. I move that the Vicar be our scribe."

"Seconded," said the Laird.

"Carried," Beauchamp declared. "Right: what will this book

26

contain? We've got an intrepid hero, so presumably we want to pit him against a dastardly villain."

"Absolutely," Ogden said. "A Russian, of course."

"Obviously," said the Laird. "A Soviet masterspy—elusive, shadowy—"

"Swarthy," Beauchamp laughed. "Mustachioed."

"A master of disguise," said the Vicar.

"Oh, yes!" Ogden enthused. "What do we call him?"

They thought about this in silence for a few minutes. Sybil left the room in disgust, which raised no objection from the others. Finally, Beauchamp said, "Do you remember that little squirt at the Soviet Embassy here in London—that translator with a lisp . . ."

"I remember him," the Laird nodded. "He had an affair with a woman at the French Embassy. We thought he was a KGB man pumping her for secrets. Turned out that she was the agent, and he was just a harmless little desk-wallah."

"How did that business finish?" Ogden said.

"She got nothing out of him, and he was shipped home when his people found out."

"Siberia?"

"Don't think so. Just out of harm's reach. Sad little chap. Anyway, does anyone remember his name?"

"Akhmatov," said the Vicar. "Yevgeny Akhmatov."

"That's the chap," Beauchamp said. "Good name for a villain."

"I agree," Ogden said. "Akhmatov it is. If he's still alive, we'll send him a copy of the book. Now, what about the stories?"

"As you said, Clive, we want plenty of violence."

"And sex," urged the Vicar. "Must have sex."

The Laird raised his pipe-stem.

"A seductive female double-agent," he said.

"Spot on," Beauchamp agreed. "Another Mata Hari."

"Desperately in love with our hero," Ogden said.

"And equally in love with the villain," said the Vicar. "Loyalties torn in two."

Ogden clapped his hands appreciatively.

"Marvellous," he declared. "This is going to work. You know chaps, I think we missed our true vocation."

FIVE

"That'll do for now," Ogden declared.

"But we've barely started," said the Vicar.

"It's enough," Ogden said. "With this lot, we should be able to find a publisher. If they like it, we'll give 'em some more."

They had been hard at work for two weeks, and the product of their labours now ran to sixty sheets of typescript. Sybil had expected them to give up after three days when the Vicar's artificial hip began to give him trouble, and Ogden broke his dentures. But to her surprise and chagrin, the friends carried on all the same, and they now had something to show for their persistence.

"Read out the opening page, Vicar," Beauchamp suggested.

"All right. Where's it gone? Ah, here we are."

The Vicar put on his spectacles, and read out the following:

"Officially, I was stationed in Berlin. In fact, my work took me much further afield. I had been seconded from MI5 to the newly-formed VO5 unit, under the auspices of Allied Joint Military Intelligence. Our brief was straightforward: to track down a string of recently-formed Soviet espionage networks operating at the highest levels in Allied military bases throughout Europe."

"Good stuff," said the Laird.

"A fine, no-nonsense opening," Ogden said.

"Absolute garbage," Sybil said.

"Carry on, Vicar."

"Our sources indicated that the whole operation, which we had code-named AARDVARK, was masterminded by one individual: an elusive figure called Yevgeny Akhmatov. We had few hard facts about Akhmatov: some said he was an *émigré* count who had been weaned back into the Soviet fold, and had spent the war returning high-grade Intelligence from the German occupied zone; others said he was not Russian at all, but a brilliant Norwegian mercenary who ran the entire AARDVARK set-up from a hut in the Pyrenees."

"Even better," Beauchamp nodded. "The sense of mystery— the exotic locations—I think we've excelled ourselves."

"Oh, for heaven's sake," Sybil groaned.

"More," commanded the Laird. "More."

"Of one thing we were certain: whoever he was, Akhmatov was ruthlessly efficient. The few people who could offer us meagre crumbs of information about Akhmatov's activities were usually murdered soon afterwards. Their bodies would be found floating in rivers, with their legs sawn off and tongues ripped out. The message was simple: informers could not hope to escape."

Sybil's lip curled in distaste.

"Is that absolutely necessary?" she asked.

"But of course," said the Vicar. "Sex and violence: it's the done thing, you know."

"And that was the violence, was it?" Sybil frowned. "What about the sex?"

"Coming right up," Ogden beamed. "Proceed, Vicar."

"But Akhmatov had one fatal weakness: women, and it was here we might hope to trap him. His sexual prowess was legendary, but it had led him into some close scrapes. One of our best informants was a French film actress whom Akhmatov had seduced and subsequently abandoned. She had turned for consolation to an Egyptian air-force pilot through whom we were able to obtain some vital clues about Akhmatov's personal habits. It emerged that Akhmatov was between forty and fifty, small in stature, powerfully built, with greasy dark hair and a swarthy, mustachioed complexion. A livid scar ran from his elbow to the palm of his right hand, the result of a student duel. A shrapnel wound gave him a slight limp and still caused him occasional discomfort which he would soothe by consuming large quantities of

Dutch gin or, when this was not available, Benedictine. He was a master of disguise, an accomplished marksman, an expert with explosives, and a brilliant exponent of clandestine radio communication."

"What a build-up!" exclaimed the Laird. "It's irresistible."
"Well, I can resist it," Sybil sniffed.
"Sybil dearest," Ogden smiled sweetly, "you could resist a panzer division. Encore, Vicar."

"Through the AARDVARK network, Akhmatov had already secured the formula for the newly-developed KP508 radar surveillance system, secret plans for the latest American high-altitude reconnaissance aircraft, and the specifications of any number of ground-to-air and anti-tank missiles. On top of all this, several networks of Allied agents throughout Eastern Europe had been exposed and liquidated: first the 69H network in Romania in late 1953, then the DDT75 network in Bulgaria in January 1954, and the RU12 ring in Poland in September of the same year. AARDVARK and Akhamatov had to be found without delay."

"That's enough," Sybil shuddered. "I think that has to be the most preposterous, cliché-ridden—"
"But it's all true," Ogden broke in.
"What?"
"You heard me. This is history."
"Nonsense. You've made it all up."
"Oh no we haven't," Ogden said firmly.
"You said you would," Sybil countered. "You decided at the very beginning that you were going to invent it all."
"We changed our minds," Ogden said. "This is all true."
"You're having me on," Sybil said.
"Not at all," Ogden insisted.
"You mean . . . there really was a—I can't believe it."
A note of doubt had crept into Sybil's voice. She picked up the typescript and read the first page.
"But it's so laughably implausible," she complained.
"History often is," Ogden said piously, and he blew a massive purple gum-ball.

Sybil stared, and shook her head.

"Well, well," she said. "I'd never have guessed it. But Godfrey, why didn't you ever tell me about a man called Akhmatov?"

The Vicar gazed at his wife reprovingly.

"Really, Sybil. I was a professional, you know."

For once, Sybil was quite nonplussed.

"Yes, but . . . Well, if you say it's true, I suppose it must be."

Ogden clapped his hands in triumph.

"Precisely!" he roared. "And if you say that, so will everyone else. Publishers, readers, the lot."

Sybil's eyes popped.

"You—you mean you were having me on?"

"Of course we were, old girl. And you swallowed it. And so will everyone else."

Sybil's face turned an interested shade of violet. She got to her feet, put her hands on her hips, and shook with rage.

"Clive Ogden," she said, in a voice quivering with indignation, "that was an unspeakable thing to do."

"Oh, steady on, Sybil," Ogden laughed. "I was just making a point."

Sybil tramped out of the room, leaving the men to weep with laughter.

"Oh dear," Ogden gasped. "I am most dreadfully sorry, Vicar."

"Not to worry," the Vicar chortled. "She'll get over it. And you did prove your point. They'll believe us, all right."

"What now?" Beauchamp said, as he blew his nose. "Find a publisher, I suppose."

"No," said the Laird. "We need an agent. I only know of one . . ."

"Is he any good?"

"It's a woman, and I've no idea. She handled Greg Bliss's book on fly fishing. He thought very highly of her."

Ogden shrugged.

"Can't hurt to have a word with her, I suppose."

As agreed, the Laird got in touch with the agent, a formidable lady called Olive Chambers, who was most impressed with the sample chapters. When she had signalled her enthusiasm to the

Laird, a meeting with all the writers was arranged one Friday morning in her office.

"Good Lord," Ogden whispered, as he entered her study. "She's even older than we are."

"Shut up," the Laird hissed.

But Ogden was quite right: Miss Chambers pre-dated her prospective clients by at least ten years. She was a corrugated, beefy old lady, with pince-nez and wiry white hair drawn back into a bun. But, as Ogden later observed, she was "still all there", and her handshake was strong enough to crack nuts.

"Mr Ogden," she smiled, "I've been looking forward to meeting you. Your memoirs are so very exciting."

Ogden shrugged nonchalantly.

"Do you think so?"

"Oh yes," she said. "Quite thrilling. It's got everything, you see: blood and thunder, betrayal and intrigue. I loved it. And these other gentlemen are . . . ?"

"Mr Croft and Mr Beauchamp. They and Mr Buchanan are my co-authors."

"Four of you?"

"That's right," Ogden said. "I'm not much of a wordsmith, you see."

"I understand," Miss Chambers said. "Men of action are seldom also men of words. Well, gentlemen, I think we have a winner here. Of course, the legal situation being what it is in this country, I don't think we shall find a British publisher. But I'm sure the Americans will be most impressed. And then there is the matter of paperbacks, translation, newspaper-serialisation rights—"

"Yes indeed," said the Laird. "We wanted to discuss that. You see, we have something a little different in mind."

"Oh?"

"We'd like the memoirs to be serialised *before* the book is published."

Miss Chambers tilted her head to one side and squinted.

"Why?"

"Well, we still haven't decided how much to write. There could be enough material for several volumes—we just don't know yet. So if we keep on producing the stuff in instalments, for publication in serial form—"

"You could publish collections every year or so."

"Precisely," Ogden said. "Can that be done?"

"I don't see why not," Miss Chambers said. "Leave it with me, and I'll see what can be arranged."

"Splendid," said the Vicar.

"I do have one small query," Miss Chambers said. "It's quite silly, really, but . . ."

"Fire away," Ogden said.

"I've read quite a few books on this general subject over the years. But I've never come across any of the names you mention: this Akhmatov fellow, for instance. And some of the organisations you name . . . well, they're entirely new to me. Why do you suppose I've never heard of them?"

Ogden smiled knowingly.

"That," he said, "gives you some idea of the level of secrecy I used to work in. This isn't your standard kiss-and-tell tittle-tattle, Miss Chambers. This stuff is red-hot, even after thirty-five years."

"My word!" Miss Chambers gasped.

"You can take it from us," Beauchamp added, "we're taking a hell of a risk publishing this material."

Miss Chambers brought her hands together and gasped.

"Gosh," she breathed. "How terribly exciting."

SIX

It was one o'clock in the morning, and Paris was beginning to quieten down. There was still traffic on the streets, but the pavements were almost deserted. The man crossed over the Pont Neuf, casting an indifferent glance towards the Conciergerie and Notre-Dame as he did so. Down below, the river Seine shimmered like a long, cold, oil slick.

As he arrived on the Left Bank, the man stopped and looked down at the river-path. It was too dark to make anything out. He found a flight of stone steps and he descended it slowly, allowing his eyes to adjust to the gloom. By the time he reached the river-path, he could see clearly enough to be sure that he was alone. The man lit a cigarette and waited.

About ten minutes later, another figure came down the steps, and stopped at the bottom. The man approached him slowly, and said, "My name's Hopkins. Are you the guy who called?"

The other man nodded, and said nothing.

"I'm glad you rang," Hopkins said. "I was planning to leave Paris tomorrow. To be honest, I've not had much luck with my inquiries. So, what have you got for me?"

The man did not reply. Suddenly, and without warning, the darkness was lit up by a dazzling white light. A *bateau mouche*, one of the Seine's sightseeing boats, swept past. Both men stood still until it had vanished, and darkness returned.

"Look," Hopkins said, "I'm not the police. I promise anything you tell me will be in confidence. What do you know about Lemiers?"

The other man spoke in a whisper: "You shall seek those who contend with you, but you shall not find them."

"What does that mean? I know Lemiers has vanished, if that's what you're saying. Do you know where he is?"

The other man laughed quietly.

"All right," Hopkins said, "if it makes it easier for you, I'm

34

willing to pay for anything you can tell me. How does that sound?"

The other man seemed to find this even more amusing.

"A soft tongue will break a bone," he chuckled.

Hopkins frowned.

"I'm not here to play games," he said. "You called me, remember. You sounded pretty anxious to talk. What's changed your mind?"

The other man sighed bitterly.

"I see that thou art in the gall of bitterness and in the bond of iniquity," he said.

Hopkins' shoulders sagged wearily.

"That's all I need," he complained. "A crank. Well, if you don't mind, I'll be moving on. It's been a long day."

He began to walk away, but the other man grabbed his sleeve. Hopkins turned round, and caught the full force of the man's fist as it ploughed into his crotch. He sank to the ground, and the other man drove his knee into Hopkins' face.

"Stop it, please," Hopkins gasped. "Look, I don't know who you are, but you're making a mistake. I'm just working for someone—"

"A servant?"

"Yes," Hopkins said. "I'm just—"

The man took hold of Hopkins' hair and pulled his head back. Then, with one movement, he brought his elbow down onto Hopkins' throat. Hopkins fell limply back onto the ground. Without pausing, the other man took out a length of cord and tied together Hopkins' hands and feet. He then rolled the body over to the edge of the path.

"Cast the worthless servant into the outer darkness," the other man quoted. "There men will weep and gnash their teeth."

With one sharp kick, the body was sent spinning into the Seine. The man watched contentedly as it slowly vanished into the inky water.

SEVEN

Miss Chambers' excitement quickly circulated among her contacts, and within weeks she had organised precisely the sort of serialisation deal her clients had requested. An American newspaper called the *Baltimore Bugle* offered an impressive sum for the right to publish and syndicate the memoirs in twice-weekly instalments.

The editor and proprietor of the *Bugle*, a Mr Cyrus X. Stompfweiner III, was deeply impressed by Clive Ogden's curriculum vitae. He telephoned the old spy to offer him his congratulations on "such a distinguished and heroic career devoted to the preservation of our great system of individual liberty and free enterprise."

"My gosh," Ogden replied. "Can't say I ever thought of it in those terms."

"You didn't?" Mr Stompfweiner said.

"Well," Ogden said quickly, "I suppose I just took all that kind of thing for granted."

"Sure you did," Mr Stompfweiner chuckled. "Anyway, Mr Ogden—can I call you Clive?"

"By all means," Ogden said graciously.

"Clive, I can only add that I consider it a privilege to be the first to bring your spectacular career to the world's attention. You're an unsung hero, Clive, and I will be the first to sing your song—"

"Jolly good," Ogden grinned.

"A Galahad in the fight against the Red Menace—"

"Good Lord—I mean, do you really think so?"

"I certainly do, Clive. And I tell you this: I would consider it an even greater privilege if at some stage you and I could actually meet and shake hands and—what was that?"

Mr Stompfweiner's oration had been interrupted by a loud pop as one of Ogden's gum-bubbles accidentally burst by the telephone mouthpiece. Ogden did not know what Mr Stompfweiner would make of a Galahad who chewed bubble-gum, but this was not the time to find out.

"Er—interference on the line," Ogden said hastily.

"Yeah? Well, Clive, am I right in hoping that at some stage we can meet over here, and maybe—"

"I don't see why not," Ogden said. "We could have a good chin-wag about the—um—Red Menace, what?"

"Just what I had in mind, Clive. Well, I'm sure you're a busy man, so I won't keep you any longer. Congratulations, Clive. You have my sincere respect."

"Thank you," Ogden smirked. "Cheerio."

He put the phone down and chuckled in satisfaction.

"Galahad, eh? How delightful."

Meanwhile, a hundred miles away at the Government Communications Headquarters in Cheltenham, a technician switched off a tape recorder, and looked up at his colleague, who was standing by a computer terminal.

"Dear oh dear," he grinned. "Have you found him yet?"

"I think so," his colleague said. "Listen to this: Clive Arthur Denham Ogden, Security Service, also Secret Intelligence Service. Retired 1981."

"That's our man. And it sounds as if he's publishing his memoirs."

"They're all doing it," the colleague said glumly. "Anyway, you'd think a guy with that experience would know better than to discuss the subject on an open, international phone line. He must realise we listen to them all."

"I bet he couldn't care less," his colleague replied. "Provided the bugger's out of the country before they publish, he's safe. Still, we'd better send all this on to London. There's a standing request on Ogden's file from some guy called Stringer in the Security Service."

By the following morning, the transcript of the conversation between Ogden and Mr Stompfweiner lay on Stringer's desk in Curzon Street. Needless to say, Stringer was far from pleased.

"The old piss-flap," he declared.

"Something the matter, Mr Stringer?" his secretary inquired.

"Yeah," Stringer said grimly. "That bastard Ogden's writing

37

his memoirs. Can you believe it? After all the trouble we took to warn those old cripples—you know something? I think he's done it on purpose. In fact, I'm sure he has."

He looked down at the transcript, and gritted his teeth in rage.

"You know what this arsehole of an American publisher called him? A Galahad in the fight against the Red Menace. Galahad! I'll give him fucking Galahad."

He put on his jacket and went over to the door.

"I'll be back in two hours," he said.

He left the building and drove south to Ogden's home in Blackheath. The journey took forty minutes, and Stringer spent most of it emitting blood-curdling oaths. By the time he arrived at Ogden's home, he had worked himself up into uncontrollable fury. He thumped violently against the front door, and bawled out Ogden's name at the top of his voice. Eventually, the door swung slowly open, and its owner blinked sleepily into the morning sunlight.

"Not today, thank you—oh, it's you, Swinger. What can I do for you?"

Stringer's reply consisted of a savage kick to the door, which sent Ogden tottering back into the hallway.

"Good heavens," Ogden gasped. "What on earth—"

"I asked you nicely," Stringer said, as he grabbed Ogden by the collar. "The D-G asked you nicely. Looks like we were pissing in the wind, doesn't it?"

"What are you talking about?" Ogden gurgled.

"You know fucking well," Stringer roared. "You're printing your memoirs, aren't you?"

"There's no need for—"

"Oh yes there is," Stringer said, as he brought his heel down hard onto Ogden's slippered foot. "There's every need. You did it on purpose, didn't you? You and your American newspaper."

He jabbed his fist into Ogden's stomach, and as the old man slumped forward, Stringer pounded Ogden's face with heavy, rhythmical slaps.

"*That's* for ignoring me," Stringer said. "*That's* for ignoring the D-G. *That's* for trying to wind us up. And *that's* for thinking you could get away with it, you stupid old twat."

Apart from a few muffled grunts, Ogden did not emit a sound.

38

When Stringer had finished, he pinned Ogden to the wall and hissed into his face: "Perhaps you'll listen this time. I want you to tear up those memoirs. I want you to phone the American, and your agent, and anyone else involved, and tell them it's all off. Otherwise, I'll come back and tear your goolies off. Get me?"

Despite his acute discomfort, Ogden forced himself to smile.

"You know, Springer old boy," he gasped, "you really do have the most awful breath. I hate to mention it, but if you will insist on panting all over a chap's face—"

Stringer grabbed what little remained of Ogden's hair, and cracked his head against the wall.

"Not funny," Stringer explained. "Now, are you going to do as I say?"

"Since—since you put it so nicely," Ogden said, "I really have no choice—"

"You haven't," Stringer agreed.

"—but to tell you to go hang."

Stringer brought up his knee into Ogden's crotch, which produced a high-pitched whimper from the old man. For half a minute, Ogden's eyes screwed up in pain. Then they slowly opened, releasing a stream of tears. Stringer grinned in satisfaction, and let Ogden fall to the ground.

"It can get a lot worse," Stringer advised him. "I'm told that at your time of life, broken bones take a long time to heal. If you don't want to spend your twilight years munching hospital food, you'd better bear that in mind."

"You can't fool me, Slinger," Ogden said weakly. "I know you're just a big softie underneath."

Stringer shook his head and planted a farewell kick in Ogden's side.

"Not funny," he repeated. "And if those memoirs appear, I'll be back."

He slammed the door behind him, and drove away. After a long interval, Ogden managed to return to his feet and hobble over to the telephone. Twenty minutes later, the Vicar and Sybil arrived with a first-aid kit, including a half-bottle of brandy.

"Well, what did you expect?" Sybil said, as she dabbed iodine on Ogden's temple.

"Nothing quite so aggressive," Ogden admitted, as he gratefully sipped the cognac. "I believe that's what's known as a hard sell."

"What a thoroughgoing brute," said the Vicar. "Fancy doing that to a man twice his age."

"A nuisance twice his age," Sybil corrected him. "That's the point. And he was right: they did warn you."

"Sybil darling," Ogden groaned, "you are such a comfort in times of stress. It's good to know that, whatever one's problems, you will offer your full support—"

"Rot," Sybil said. "You asked for it, and he gave it to you. And if you've any sense at all, you'll do as he says. Now, where else did he hurt you?"

"Well," Ogden mused, "I've got some nasty bruises on my toe, my hip, and my unmentionables. The toe and the hip will sort themselves out, but if you fancy administering some massage to—"

"Don't be absurd," Sybil snapped. "You can deal with that yourself."

"I suppose it's all over," the Vicar observed.

"What is?"

"You know, the memoirs. We can't really go ahead now, can we?"

Ogden stared in surprise.

"Why on earth not?"

The Vicar scratched his head in bewilderment.

"But—but—after all this—"

"What of it?" Ogden said. "You don't seriously think I'm going to give in to some street-corner hoodlum, do you?"

Sybil shook her head in disgust.

"You're incorrigible," she said.

"Absolutely," Ogden agreed. "I don't give in to bullies. Never have, never will."

"But he'll hospitalise you."

"He won't dare," Ogden said. "Think about it: once the memoirs are printed, I'll be a public figure. If I'm knocked about, it will be pretty bad publicity for MI5, not to mention Her Majesty's Government. No, the moment we're published we'll be safe as houses."

"You really believe that?" Sybil said incredulously.

"Of course," Ogden said. "Why do you think Stinger cut up so rough this morning? Impotent rage. The act of a desperate man."

"An utter brute," the Vicar agreed. "Still, what do you expect from a man who plays football?"

EIGHT

And so, despite Stringer's threats, the following Wednesday's edition of the *Baltimore Bugle* carried the first instalment of Clive Ogden's memoirs under the heading, "Stranger than fiction—the sensational, uncensored autobiography of a British secret agent."

There was considerable reaction in the United States; other newspapers and television stations expressed varying degrees of incredulity about Ogden's spectacular career. "Clive Ogden: Superspy or Superfraud?" asked one paper. Another insisted that "Ogden, like his arch-enemy Akhmatov, is a B-movie invention." The *Washington Post* insisted that Ogden was "the espionage world's answer to Baron Munchausen", but the *Los Angeles Times* was more noncommittal, urging that judgment be suspended until the British government issued a statement. *The Times'* caution perhaps owed more to commerce than objectivity: it too was running the memoirs.

Not surprisingly, the British Press's initial coverage was slight. The first stories appeared on the second or back pages of the newspapers, merely stating that a new espionage autobiography had appeared in the United States, and that the Government had so far delayed commenting upon its contents. Clearly, the media world was waiting for the official reaction to Ogden's extraordinary tales before making up its mind.

The reaction, when it came, was everything Ogden and his friends had hoped for. MPs of various parties had tabled questions about the memoirs in the House of Commons, and Ogden & Co. listened to the radio as the Home Secretary issued his statement: "In reply to the Honourable Member for Sevenoaks, I can confirm that Mr Ogden is indeed a former member of the security services, though I am not prepared to reveal the specific nature of his employment there."

"Good man," Ogden nodded. "Keep it vague."

"Nor," said the Home Secretary, "am I prepared to answer

questions about any specific claims and allegations in his memoirs. The House is fully aware that our policy is neither to confirm or deny such claims—"

The House burst into an incredulous uproar, and Ogden rubbed his hands gleefully.

"Splendid," he said. "Just what the doctor ordered."

"The bloody fool," said the Laird. "Doesn't he realise—?"

"I can only add," said the Home Secretary, "that we greatly deplore the publication of any such memoirs from Crown Servants, who have a lifelong duty of confidentiality concerning all aspects of their employment."

"Extraordinary!" the Vicar exclaimed. "He's as good as confirmed our stories."

"What did I tell you?" Ogden grinned.

"Furthermore," said the Home Secretary, "the House will be pleased to hear that the Attorney-General has been granted an injunction banning the publication of these memoirs in Great Britain, and he is now considering what further action, if any, he will take."

"I knew it," Sybil muttered. "You'll be arrested and sent to prison, and you can't say I didn't—"

"Nonsense," Ogden laughed. "He can't touch us. You wait and see."

When the Home Secretary had sat down, the MPs pelted him with questions.

"Surely," one said, "it could do no harm whatsoever to national security for the Home Secretary to confirm that these so-called memoirs are just a tissue of lies, written solely for profit."

"Bloody cheek!" Beauchamp said indignantly.

"Don't worry," Ogden said. "He won't let us down."

"I deeply regret," the Home Secretary said, "that I am unable to give the House such confirmation. As I have already explained, we do not, under any circumstances, make comment upon leaked or illicit material relating to state security."

The House was not pleased by this, and it expressed its displeasure with its customary barrage of hoots, groans and catcalls.

"Splendid fellow," the Vicar smiled. "Don't give in."

"He won't," said the Laird.

And he didn't. After a number of similar questions failed to elicit any response from the Home Secretary, the MPs changed tack, and demanded that terrible punishments be visited upon Ogden immediately. But here too, the Home Secretary was remarkably vague: he repeated that the Attorney-General was looking into the matter, and that the House must await his decision. Of course, no MP was to know that prosecution had already been ruled out by the Attorney-General, for the very reasons Ogden had given to his friends: the memoirs were, in effect, a work of fiction, and contained nothing that could be described as an official secret.

The net result was precisely what Ogden had anticipated: the papers which carried the old spy's memoirs now sold in huge numbers, and the issue became international front-page news. With some embarrassment, the *Washington Post* was forced to withdraw some of its unkinder remarks about Ogden.

"Is it possible," the newspaper inquired, "that these fantastic exploits really occurred? Did Ogden really have a life-or-death knife-fight at the top of the Eiffel tower with a Bulgarian spy? Did Yevgeny Akhmatov really conceal a miniature camera in his cuff-link? Did Sylvia von Hubschen really smuggle atomic secrets in her brassière? After the British Home Secretary's performance in Parliament, we must now give these amazing stories serious consideration."

With a note of relief, the *Los Angeles Times* ran a "we-told-you-so" editorial: "Truth *is* stranger than fiction, and Ogden's life story merely underlines this fact. There can be no further doubt about Ogden's bona fides: the British Government has confirmed that he was one of their agents, and they do not dispute his version of events. Given the traditional British obsession with secrecy, this is the nearest we will ever get to an official confirmation that the memoirs are true."

The British Press was not in a position to discuss Ogden's veracity: under the terms of the Attorney-General's court injunction, they were forbidden to repeat any of the stories. So apart from the odd remark about "James Bond-style plots" and "Bulldog Drummond prose", they confined themselves to the question of Ogden's legal status.

Why, asked the *Daily Telegraph*, had not Ogden been summarily arrested? *The Times* began to ask similar questions, but since no reply was forthcoming from the Government, the issue looked as if it might fizzle out.

Matters were quickly put right, however, by a retired army officer named Colonel Arthur Pelham-Crabwicke. The colonel was incensed by the Government's vacillation and evasiveness on the subject of Clive Ogden, and he wrote to all the newspapers to tell them so. The colonel expressed himself in such forceful terms that almost all his letters were printed, including the following, which appeared in *The Times*:

Sir,
What has this nation come to when a dishonest, despicable blackguard like Clive Ogden can make complete fools of our authorities and go unpunished? What on earth is the Government playing at?

I met Ogden some thirty-six years ago—we used to play in the same cricket team—and even then I knew him to be a cad of the deepest dye. His sneaky, unprincipled yorkers and excessive appeals to the umpire indicated a low, unscrupulous personality, and we had no hesitation in running him out of our club. In retrospect, I feel he deserved a sound thrashing, and I wish I had administered one. Recent events have only strengthened this conviction.

It is well known that on several occasions—in Palestine, Malaya, etc.—the British authorities have found it expedient to "remove" certain subversive individuals who posed a serious threat to law and order. Perhaps it is time to revive this practice. If the nation's present servants are too weak-kneed and unpatriotic to perform such a task, I for one would be more than willing to assist with the "disappearance" of Clive Ogden.
Yours very sincerely,
Arthur Pelham-Crabwicke, R.A. (Retd.)

The colonel's letters provoked a flood of similar correspondence to the newspapers. It seemed that all over the country, retired officers were itching to wreak vengeance on Clive Ogden. The Home Secretary was compelled to make a speech in which he sympathised with the servicemen's feelings, but urged them to remain calm and not take the law into their own hands.

If Ogden felt at all uneasy about these threats of violence and murder, he kept the fact well hidden. Indeed, he seemed to find the subject highly entertaining.

"Listen to this one," he said, holding up a newspaper cutting. "'Does Ogden wear dentures? He certainly will, if I get my hands on him.' From Wing-Commander D.H.K. Medhurst. Is that one of yours, Vicar?"

"No," Beauchamp said. "I wrote it."

"Well done," Ogden giggled. "I loved the one in the *Express*: 'the Orientals had the right idea—if they talk, pull their tongues out. There should be no mercy for squealers. Admiral L. B. Smedley, R.N.'"

"That *was* mine," the Vicar said.

"Really, Godfrey," Sybil grimaced. "That's disgusting."

"Jolly funny though," the Vicar sniggered.

"But don't they check these letters?" Sybil asked. "I mean, there are lists of retired officers, aren't there?"

"Of course there are," Ogden said. "Where do you think we found all these names?"

"I wonder what the real Arthur Pelham-Crabwicke thinks of all this," the Laird said. "He must be bloody furious."

"Oh, I don't know," Ogden said. "He probably agrees with every line I wrote on his behalf. And if he doesn't—well, so what?"

"What if he complains?"

"Let him," Ogden shrugged. "It's up to the papers to vet their correspondence. I say, listen to this: 'We can begin by birching the fellow. Then, when he's black and blue and screaming for mercy, he should be made to eat every copy of his autobiography. Like your other correspondents, I would be delighted to do the job myself. We did it at Cawnpore—we can do it again.' Marvellous stuff. Who wrote it?"

"Not me," said the Laird.

"Or me," said the Vicar.

"Jeremy?"

"Afraid not," Beauchamp said.

The friends looked uneasily at each other, and Ogden dabbed his forehead with a handkerchief.

"Good Lord," he breathed. "It's a real one!"

He picked up a nearby copy of the Army List, and looked up the correspondent's name.

"Brigadier-General Rupert Fellowes . . . oh, thank heavens."

He shut the book and sighed in relief.

"Panic over, chaps. He's eighty-six."

NINE

"It's a fucking joke," Stringer said bitterly. "Have you seen this crap?"

The D-G sighed, and glanced over the relevant column of the latest *Baltimore Bugle*, which the British Embassy had obligingly sent over by fax.

"Christ," he muttered. "Listen to this: 'Krauss slashed the knife down towards my head with terrifying speed. I reached up and caught his wrist in the nick of time—the blade stopped just millimetres from my throat. Then, with one sharp twist, I broke his arm.' How can anyone believe this garbage?"

"But they do," Stringer said.

The D-G screwed up the article and tossed it into his wastepaper basket.

"Of course," he said, "our friends think it's hilarious. The CIA Director telexed me to ask if Ogden could be brought out of retirement to take a few pictures of some Soviet missile silo."

"Fucking Yanks," Stringer groaned.

"And ASIO told us they think Ogden was a Soviet infiltrator, because he's smarter than any pommie spy they've ever heard of."

"Ha bloody ha ha."

"Unfortunately," the D-G said, "it's getting beyond a joke."

He picked up a wad of notes and memos from his desk.

"From the Foreign Office. The Home Office. Even the PM. Basically, they all say the same thing: what the hell are we doing about Ogden?"

Stringer shook his head.

"I don't get it," he said. "I thought the Attorney-General was cooking something up."

"That was just for public consumption. The Law Officers are adamant: any prosecution they brought would almost certainly be thrown out immediately. And even if they could find an amenable judge, no jury would ever convict. The Government

48

would just get even more egg on its face. No, they insist the ball's back in our court."

"And what are we supposed to do? Take Ogden out, like that Colonel suggested?"

The D-G's face screwed up in disgust.

"That was another hoax," he said. "All those letters were written by Ogden and his cronies."

"I might have bloody known," Stringer cried. "Jesus Christ, I thought old people were supposed to behave responsibly."

"Well," the D-G said, "they call it second childhood, don't they? Look at the way Ogden chews that bubble-gum. Quite pathetic. But unfortunately, these toddlers are making a hell of a nuisance of themselves. So, what do we propose to do about them?"

Stringer shrugged.

"I could pay another visit to Ogden, I guess. The last call wasn't good enough to persuade him, so we'll have to do it properly this time. If we broke all the fingers in his writing hand, and maybe his leg as well, he might start to get the message."

The D-G shook his head.

"Out of the question. He's news now."

"All right—how about threatening a relative?"

"Possible," said the D-G. "Anyone suitable?"

"Just a daughter in New Zealand. Married, with a baby son. Ogden's never seen his grandchild, but he still wouldn't like it if we—"

"No," said the D-G. "New Zealand's too risky. If anything went wrong, the natives would crucify us. Remember those frogs who blew up the Greenpeace ship. Are there no other relations?"

"None we could find," Stringer said. "There are some friends, but none are close enough to assure us of leverage. Except, of course, for Croft, Beauchamp and Buchanan—but Ogden has made it known that they're his co-authors."

"In that case, we'd better rule out the heavy stuff. For the time being, at any rate."

Stringer lit a cigarette and tossed the match into the D-G's ashtray.

"What's left?" he said.

The D-G leaned back in his chair and thought about it. After a couple of minutes, he made up his mind.

"There's only one thing we can do," he decided. "Discredit the memoirs."

Stringer gave a sardonic laugh.

"That shouldn't be hard. The bloody thing discredits itself."

"No, you're missing my point. The only reason Ogden's getting so much publicity is because the Government can't officially deny his stories. Well, unofficially it's another matter. I see no reason why we can't give an off-the-record Press briefing, and explain that these so-called memoirs are all made up."

"I don't like it," Stringer said. "If that's all that's needed, why hasn't Downing Street done it already? They hand out unattributable briefings like confetti."

"They're too close to this one," the D-G said. "The PM has made this confidentiality business an issue of principle. But we haven't, and if something goes wrong, Downing Street can truthfully claim they know nothing about it."

Stringer frowned pensively and blew out a long cloud of smoke.

"I'm still not crazy about the idea," he said.

"Nor am I," the D-G admitted. "But can you improve on it?"

"Not off-hand," Stringer said.

"Good," said the D-G. "In that case, would you mind organising it?"

He glanced at his desk diary.

"Let's say Friday morning."

"Why not?" Stringer shrugged.

TEN

"You know, Vicar," Beauchamp said, "this really is a nice piece."

He was examining the antique clock above the mantelpiece in the Vicar's drawing-room.

"Yes," the Vicar said. "It is quite pretty, isn't it?"

"I never really looked at it before. Eighteenth-century French. Very good condition."

"Careful, Vicar," said the Laird. "I see dollar-signs in Jeremy's eyes."

"If he names a price," Ogden advised, "insist on ten times more."

"It was my grandmother's," Sybil said warily. "And I'm not interested in its cash value. It has great sentimental—"

"I was just curious," Beauchamp said.

He took the clock down and examined it closely.

"As I thought. A boulle bracket clock by Roquelon of Paris. You know, this is quite rare."

Sybil's haughtiness melted slightly.

"Is it very—I mean, is it greatly sought after?"

"I'd say so," Beauchamp said. "It would fetch a very good price. Five, six thousand. Perhaps more."

"My word," said the Vicar. "We had no idea."

Sybil's eyes widened, and she gazed at the clock with a new fascination.

"I never realised—I mean, I knew it was valuable, but . . . Jeremy, do you know anything about jewellery?"

"A little," Beauchamp said.

"You see, Grandma left me some of her things: brooches, rings, and a few lockets . . ."

"Let's see 'em," Beauchamp said.

The possibility of unexpected wealth took twenty years off Sybil, and she scuttled upstairs with girlish speed.

"You're not pulling her leg, are you, Jeremy?" the Vicar said anxiously. "She'll only take it out on me."

"I don't joke about antiques," Beauchamp sniffed.

"Never mind all that," Ogden said. "Have you read this morning's papers? It says here that 'security sources' have made it known that my memoirs are a fantasy, and that I was just an MI5 paper-pusher."

"Aha," said the Laird. "I wondered what their next move would be."

"How did they arrange that?" asked the Vicar.

"An unattributable briefing," Beauchamp said. "I once gave one of those. It's quite handy, really. The Press are such sheep, they'll believe anything you tell them, providing it comes with a nod and a wink."

"So that's it, then," the Laird said. "The game's up."

"What do you mean?"

"Well, we've been exposed, haven't we? Now everyone knows."

"Nonsense," Ogden said.

"But if MI5 have rubbished the memoirs—"

"They've *tried* to rubbish them," Ogden said. "They haven't necessarily succeeded."

"What do you mean?"

"Look," Ogden said patiently, "suppose the memoirs were genuine—"

"But they're not."

"Suppose they were. What would MI5 do?"

"Precisely the same thing," said the Vicar. "They'd hold a briefing and deny their authenticity."

"Exactly," Ogden smiled. "So who's going to believe them?"

"Our newspapers, for a start."

Ogden waved his hand dismissively.

"They don't count," he said. "All that should concern us is what the Americans think. And I expect them to be a little less gullible than our people."

He glanced at his watch.

"The American papers should all be out by now. Miss Chambers said she would phone me with their reaction as soon as she heard."

Sybil returned with her jewellery box, which she handed to Beauchamp.

"There's one brooch in particular," she said, "which I'm sure is very—er—rare."

Sybil would never bring herself to utter words such as "valuable" or "expensive" in this context.

"This one?" Beauchamp said.

He drew out a brooch with matching earrings. They were made of gold and amethyst, and Beauchamp virtually salivated over them.

"Gorgeous," he declared. "1840 to 1850. Immaculate. Worth at least a thousand—"

Before Sybil could react to this news, the phone rang, and she went to answer it.

"Hello?" she barked. "Yes, he's here."

She thrust the receiver at Ogden as if it were a dagger, and turned back to Beauchamp.

"Are you quite sure about that . . . ?"

"Hello?" Ogden said. "Fine, thank you, Miss Chambers, and how are you? . . . Indeed? . . . Yes, by all means."

Ogden produced a note-pad from his pocket and took down Miss Chambers' dictation. When she had finished, he chuckled and said, "Yes, it's excellent news. Thank you for calling, Miss Chambers. Cheerio."

"Well?" the Laird demanded.

"As I expected," Ogden beamed. "The Yanks aren't having any of it. If anything, MI5's behaviour has strengthened their belief in the truth of my memoirs."

"Splendid," said the Vicar.

The Laird blew out a long, thoughtful cloud of pipe-smoke.

"You know what?" he said. "I think we should send another letter to the newspapers from a retired serviceman. 'Dear Sir— why are MI5 pussyfooting around? What is the point of issuing lame denials, which nobody will believe, when the real answer is to drag Ogden out and give him a public birching? Yours, etc.'"

"Definitely," Ogden nodded. "Furthermore, we should—"

The phone rang once more. Sybil gave an impatient hiss and snatched up the receiver.

"Yes? One moment. It's for you again, Clive."

"Really?" Ogden blinked. "I wasn't expecting any further calls. Hello?"

An unfamiliar, muffled voice came down the line.

"Mr Ogden? Please listen. I'm in a call-box with little change, so please don't interrupt. I have been reading your memoirs, and I think you could offer me help in a very delicate matter concerning a mutual friend—"

"Who's that?"

"Not now, Mr Ogden. Can I meet you tomorrow? Somewhere discreet. Outdoors, preferably."

"Well—I suppose—"

"It's very important, Mr Ogden, and you're the only person I know who can help."

"Am I?" Ogden blinked.

"I think so."

"How did you know I was here?"

"I guessed. Mr Croft's name was linked to yours in a newspaper article, and his number is in the directory. Bring him too, if he is willing to come."

"Oh, very well," Ogden said. "Shall we say Wandsworth Common, at three p.m. tomorrow?"

"Fine. Where on the Common?"

"By the cricket ground. We'll be on the path adjoining the tennis courts—"

"I know it."

The newspaper caught Ogden's eye, and a suspicion occurred to him.

"This isn't a hoax, is it?" he asked.

"No, Mr Ogden."

"How can I be sure?"

There was a pause at the other end of the line, and the voice said, "Do you remember Gerald Carter?"

Ogden scratched his head.

"Why, yes, I do. He was with me in—what's the matter with him?"

"He's dead. See you tomorrow, Mr Ogden."

The man hung up. Ogden put the phone down, and gazed at his colleagues in stupefaction.

"You won't believe this," he said.

"Who was it?"

"I don't know," Ogden said, and he recounted the conversation.

"A joke," said the Laird. "Has to be."

54

"Yes," Sybil said. "I definitely smell a rat."

"What does it matter?" Ogden said. "The Common's not far from here. If it is a hoax, the worst we'll suffer is a pleasant stroll."

"I'm game," Beauchamp said, and the other men nodded.

"What if it's some kind of trap?" Sybil said. "Somebody waiting to kidnap you?"

"In broad daylight?" Ogden laughed. "All three of us? I rather doubt it. And besides, there will be people playing in the tennis courts, and there'll probably be a cricket match in progress."

"You think so?" the Vicar said eagerly. "In that case, I'm definitely going."

Sybil shook her head.

"Well, I can't stop you. But if you'll take my advice, you'll stay at home."

She turned to Beauchamp and said, "Now, what do you think of this cameo?"

ELEVEN

Pieter Lemiers looked at his watch. It was quarter to eleven. He pushed his papers aside and rubbed his eyes. That was quite enough work for one day, he decided. Time to be going.

There was nobody else in the office. The last of the staff had gone home five hours before, leaving their boss alone with his books. Lemiers had an important meeting tomorrow morning: with luck, he should be able to clinch a lucrative deal for his firm. He did not propose to blow that deal through lack of preparation.

He put his papers back into their file and turned off his desk-lamp. Just as he was about to put on his jacket, his office door swung open, and a large man stepped in.

"Hello?" Lemiers said. "Who are you?"

The man ignored the question, and closed the door.

"How did you get in? It's supposed to be locked downstairs."

The man paced around Lemiers' office, like an expectant father in a maternity clinic. Lemiers was a patient man, but it was late, and his visitor's behaviour would have exasperated a Buddhist monk.

"Will you please answer my question?" he snapped.

His visitor stared indignantly at Lemiers, and wagged an admonitory finger in his direction.

"Gird up thy loins like a man," he said. "I will question thee."

Lemiers picked up the phone and dialled.

"Hello? Please get me the police."

The man ran across the office and brought his hand down onto the receiver hook. Before Lemiers had a chance to protest, the phone cable was torn out of its socket, and the instrument flung across the room.

"Because thou hast done this," the man bellowed, "cursed art thou above all wild cattle and above all wild animals. Upon thy belly thou shalt go."

He grabbed Lemiers and threw him onto the carpet.

56

"What are you doing?" Lemiers panted. "Look—if it's money you want, I think there's some in the safe—"

The man snorted in disgust, and planted a foot on Lemiers' chest.

"All right," Lemiers said. "What do you want, then? Information, perhaps?"

Lemiers tried desperately to think who this man could be. Like all successful businessmen, he had some enemies—one or two rivals, and a former partner—but none would ever send such a man to injure him. The only possibility was that this man had something to do with the Paris job. It seemed unlikely, but . . .

"Are you from Invicta?" he asked. "If you are, I swear I've got nothing to hide. Honestly, there's no secret about—"

The man seemed unimpressed.

"The secret things belong to the Lord our God," he said cryptically. "But the things that are revealed belong to us."

"The Lord?" Lemiers repeated. "Who are you? Some kind of maniac? Listen, whoever you are, you may think God's on your side, but the police certainly aren't. If you'll take my advice—"

"Who is this that darkens counsel by words without knowledge?" the man thundered. "The Lord hears when I call to him."

"Yes," Lemiers agreed desperately. "Anything you say. Now if you'll just get your foot off my chest . . ."

"'I will vent my wrath on my enemies, and avenge myself on my foes,' sayeth the Lord."

The man drew out a pistol and aimed it at Lemiers' face.

"No," Lemiers shouted. "Please—"

The man fired four times, and stepped back. He put away the gun and went to the door. Casting one last glance at Lemiers' body, he murmured, "Thus sayeth the Lord: 'The dead bodies of men shall fall like dung upon the open field.'"

And with that uplifting thought, the man turned off the light and went away.

TWELVE

"It's in the air," Ogden observed. "He must be . . ."

"Out," Beauchamp said.

"Well caught, sir," the Vicar called out.

The batsman left the crease, and Ogden & Co. applauded his innings. They were the only spectators that afternoon: it was not warm, and the sky had turned an ominous shade of sepia. Even the nearby tennis courts were unattended. The cricketers seemed mildly bemused by the four garrulous, dishevelled old men huddled together on one park bench, but they acknowledged their clapping with good grace, and returned the applause whenever Ogden blew a particularly large gum-bubble.

"He was unlucky," said the Vicar, as the new batsman took his position. "He looked to be in line for a quick fifty."

"Unlucky my foot," said the Laird. "That ball was unplayable. Hello, is this our chap?"

They turned and saw a middle-aged man in a shabby overcoat walking slowly up the path towards them. He was probably in his late fifties, but looked older: his face was of a yellowish complexion, and the deep lines around his neck suggested that he had lost a lot of weight in a hurry. There was a sad, exhausted air about him, and the friends secretly hoped that he was not their man.

"Good afternoon," he said. "Is one of you Mr Ogden?"

"That's me," Ogden nodded. "You didn't tell me your name."

"I'm sorry about that," the man replied. "Though you'll understand why, presently. I'm Jonathan Blake."

"Pleased to meet you," Ogden said, and he introduced his friends. "Now, what's all this about Gerald Carter?"

"He's been murdered," Blake said.

"Good grief," Ogden exclaimed. "Why? Who did it?"

"I don't know," Blake said. "That's why I wanted to see you. Gerald once mentioned that you worked with him in Intelligence—"

58

"That's right," Ogden nodded. "He left several years before I retired, and we didn't keep in touch. We weren't close, but I knew him reasonably well. I'm sorry to hear—well, what on earth happened?"

"It's quite a long story," Blake warned, "and I'd like you to hear it all, if you have the time."

"Fire away," said the Laird, waving his pipe. "We've nothing better to do. Shift along, chaps."

They moved along their seat, and made room for the lugubrious Mr Blake.

"Gerald and I were partners," Blake began. "We owned a company called Invicta Design and Development, based in Kent, which sold arms and security equipment. I handled domestic clients—the police mainly, and one or two gun clubs. Gerald dealt with the international side, using contacts he'd made while working in security. You must understand right away that we were a perfectly legitimate company—at least, as far as I was concerned."

"There's nothing legitimate about the international arms trade," the Vicar murmured.

"Perhaps you're right," Blake said, nodding slowly. "But that wasn't my department, and I assumed that Gerald's side of the business was as above board as my own. I suppose I was naïve.

"Anyway, some six months ago I fell ill. I won't bore you with the details, but suffice it to say that I spent a long time in hospital, and left the business in Gerald's hands. What I know about subsequent events is almost entirely second-hand—either from Gerald himself, or other people.

"While I was in hospital, Gerald was contacted by a Dutch arms dealer named Lemiers who was based in Paris, and had something to sell. He'd never heard of Lemiers before, but it's not unusual to get offers like that: names are passed around grapevines, you see, and certain companies become known for dealing in certain goods. Anyway, Lemiers seemed to know what he was talking about, and his wares were right up our street."

"What were they?" Ogden asked.

"It was quite a big load, a job lot from the Israeli government. They were offering him things like sniper rifles with day- and night-sights, and sub-machine-guns with specialised fittings, such as infra-red detection devices, targetting systems, and so forth.

59

But it wasn't just guns: there were explosives, too—grenades, mines, linear cutting charges, and things like that."

"Was he offering a good price?"

"It was very reasonable," Blake said. "If Lemiers had broken the shipment up and sold it piecemeal, he'd probably have made a bigger profit. But that would have taken a long time, and he'd have run up heavy storage charges. So he preferred to sell it all off in one go and make slightly less. Nothing unusual in that."

"How did your partner react?"

"Gerald was keen. He asked Lemiers for ten days to think it over, and the Dutchman agreed. Shortly afterwards, Gerald had lunch with one of his army contacts, a man called Brigadier Symes—"

"David Symes?"

"That's right," Blake nodded. "Do you know him?"

"Yes," Ogden said. "I worked abroad with him one time. We needed some Arab contacts, and David knows quite a few."

"He would," Blake said. "He's organised many arms deals involving Middle-Eastern governments. Anyway, Symes put a lot of business our way. Gerald used to have lunch with him once a month at the Special Forces Club in London, and Symes usually had a shopping list."

"He bought guns on behalf of our government?" Beauchamp said.

"Not exactly," Blake smiled. "There are some countries to whom the British government prefers not to be seen selling arms. Not necessarily for legal reasons; often it's just a question of public relations."

"Tinpot dictators, and the like," Ogden grinned.

"Sometimes," Blake admitted. "Anyway, in those cases, the Government puts the business our way, so the deal doesn't go to some other country. Symes' job is to put the relevant parties in touch with each other. On this occasion, the prospective client was an American ex-marine called Colonel Kyle, who ran a firm called Magnum Inc. of Colorado."

"What did this American want?"

"Machine guns and explosives," Blake said. "And Symes thought he might be interested in the sniper rifles, as well. Symes didn't know any more than that, but Gerald was keen, and Symes said he'd give Kyle our number.

"Kyle got in touch two days later. He said he was quite impressed by Gerald's package, and he'd be over the next day to discuss it."

"The next day? He *was* impressed."

"Evidently. When Gerald met him, Kyle explained that he wanted the arms quite badly, but there was a hitch: no end-user certificate."

"What does that mean?" asked the Laird.

"An end-user certificate accompanies every legal arms transaction. It proves that the final destination for the arms—the end-user—is a country, and not some private gangster. Guns can be bought and re-sold any number of times, provided they are accompanied by one of these documents."

"But Kyle didn't have one?"

"No. As I said, I assumed Gerald's side of the business was above board, and that he wouldn't dream of making an illegal transaction of that sort. Well, I was wrong. Kyle offered a big sum for the shipment—more than it was worth, I think— provided Gerald arranged the whole thing.

"Of course, Gerald was taking all the risks: if the shipment was uncovered, he would be arrested. So Kyle agreed to pay the whole fee in advance, as a sweetener. They shook hands on it, and Gerald got back onto Lemiers."

"Where did Kyle want the arms sent?"

"To his company, in the United States. Gerald explained the position to Lemiers, who seemed very understanding about the matter. Lemiers said he could obtain a forged Italian end-user cert., which would allow him to take the goods from the Israelis and ship them to Italy. The guns would then be disguised and sent to Naples, where Gerald would oversee the loading-up. Then they'd be shipped to Southampton, and transferred to another ship for the United States."

"Couldn't he find a ship heading directly to the States?"

"No," Blake said. "Gerald was Lemiers' client, and the Dutchman insisted that he should take the goods off his hands. I suppose it ensured that Gerald couldn't back off, if anything went wrong."

"I see," Beauchamp said. "And how were the arms concealed?"

"They were in special drums, disguised as chemicals: fertilisers or pesticides, or someting of that sort. Anyway, Lemiers found a ship—the SS *Flavio*—and Gerald watched the drums being put on board. The boat left Naples on the specified date, and so did Gerald. He flew home and waited for the *Flavio* at Southampton. But it never arrived."

"Aha," said the Laird. "The plot thickens."

"Gerald knew the ship would first be stopping in Gibraltar, so he phoned the port authorities there. The *Flavio* hadn't even got that far. It simply vanished."

"Well bowled!" said the Vicar.

"Naturally, Gerald tried to trace the ship," Blake said, "but he couldn't find it anywhere. So he told Colonel Kyle, who was not best pleased."

"I bet," Ogden laughed. "What did Kyle do?"

"What could he do? It was an illegal shipment, so they couldn't go to the authorities. Gerald had paid the Dutchman for the arms, so Kyle couldn't demand his money back. He just had to lump it."

"Ouch," Ogden winced.

"Exactly," Blake nodded. "Gerald hadn't lost anything, but he was still furious. If word got around that he'd been diddled so easily, nobody would do business with us. He was determined to find out what had become of the ship."

"Did he?" asked the Vicar.

"Yes and no. The *Flavio* isn't the first boat to have done a bunk with its cargo. Most of the time, the ships go to Beirut which of course hasn't been policed for years. Gerald went to the Lebanon and asked around. He couldn't get any precise details about the *Flavio*'s itinerary, but several people had spotted the ship in Turkey, and it was now rumoured to be in Cyprus. So Gerald flew over to Larnaca, but he never got a chance to look around the harbour: he checked into a hotel, and one hour later he was found dead in his room. His neck was broken."

"Christ," Ogden said. "That's—that's awful."

"The murderer wasn't found," Blake said. "The police said there were no clues worth mentioning, but I don't think they were particularly interested."

"And what did you do?" the Laird asked.

Blake sighed.

"The best I could," he said, "which wasn't much. I discharged myself from hospital and began my own inquiries. I was too ill to travel, so I hired a private investigator—a man called Hopkins— to find out what the hell was going on. Hopkins flew to Larnaca, and got nowhere. So he tried to find Lemiers, to see if he knew anything. It turned out that Lemiers' Paris office was just an empty apartment, and the phone line was disconnected. Hopkins asked around to see if anyone had heard of Lemiers, and it transpired that he was a complete unknown in the arms world. It was as if he had never existed."

"What about the Israelis? They had sold Lemiers the arms in the first place, hadn't they?"

"They denied all knowledge of him," Blake said. "And they were adamant that they hadn't sold any arms of the kind we described."

"Maybe they were lying," Beauchamp suggested.

"I don't think so. There was no reason to lie to me—we were a reputable firm, and the alleged transaction with Lemiers was perfectly in order. No, I think they were telling the truth: wherever the arms came from, it wasn't Israel."

"What happened next?"

"Things got even worse," Blake said. "Hopkins went quiet for a week, and I began to get worried. His last call was from Paris, and when I contacted the police there, I found that he too had been murdered, and dumped in the Seine."

Ogden and his friends gazed at each other uneasily.

"It's a nasty little tale, isn't it?" the Vicar observed.

Blake looked down at the ground.

"I tried to get in touch with Colonel Kyle. His company has ceased trading, and nobody knows where he is. My last clue was Brigadier Symes, and he's unavailable. No one will say where he is."

"For heaven's sake, why?"

"I don't know. But I think our authorities know a lot more about all this than they're prepared to admit. The Foreign Office claims to be looking into this business, but they certainly haven't made it their top priority. At first I thought they just regarded me as a nuisance. Now I suspect it's more serious than that."

"What makes you think so?"

"I'm almost certain that my phone's being tapped," Blake said. "Several times in my inquiries, I've phoned people for help. At first they were happy to see me, and we'd fix appointments. But minutes later they'd get back to me and cancel, for no proper reason. Not hours later, mind, but *minutes*."

"You think they were got at?"

"I'm sure of it. And that means the authorities are keeping an eye on me. Why? What the hell is going on?"

"Is that why you phoned me from a call-box, without giving your name?" Ogden said.

"Yes. You see, Gerald fixed the shipment through an old Intelligence contact—Symes. Now the Intelligence people are tapping my phone, or so I suspect. It seems to me that the only people who could get to the bottom of this are other Intelligence people. I've tried contacting all the ex-colleagues Gerald mentioned to me. All of them have refused to have anything to do with me, for the reasons I've explained.

"You were the only one left, and I didn't know how to reach you. Then I heard about your memoirs, and I found Mr Croft's name in the directory."

"I see," Ogden said. "So what would you like us to do for you?"

"Firstly," Blake said, "you could find out if my phone really is being tapped. If it isn't, and I'm just being paranoid, that's the end of the matter. But if I'm right, it will mean the authorities are involved, and you might be able to discover why."

The friends glanced at each other again, but Ogden now looked doubtful.

"I'd love to help," he said. "But I'm not sure how we could find out if you're being tapped. We're not exactly flavour of the month in MI5, you know . . ."

"To be more accurate," said the Laird, "our name is mud, and they'd sooner entrust us with the Crown Jewels than their precious tapping list."

"We're probably on it ourselves," Beauchamp grinned.

"We don't need it," the Vicar said. "There are other ways."

"Ah," Ogden grinned. "There speaks the expert. The Vicar used to work in telecom interception, Mr Blake, so listen carefully."

"It all depends," said the Vicar. "Mr Blake, do you know if your local telephone exchange has been modernised? They're all going over to the new digital System X nowadays, you see, but they tell the clients when they've done it. Have you had notification of that? It usually comes with your phone bill."

"No," Blake said. "I don't recall anything like that. I live in a rural part of Kent, you see . . ."

"Good, good," said the Vicar. "In that case, we're in with a chance. Give us a week, and we'll tell you if you're being tapped."

"Can you do it that soon?"

"Oh yes," the Vicar said confidently. "We'll need some money, I'm afraid."

"I haven't much," Blake admitted. "A few thousand, at most."

"Oh, we don't need *that* much," the Vicar smiled. "A few hundred will do, and you'll get most of it back. It's a relatively simple job."

"If you say so, Vicar," Ogden frowned. "But—"

"I do say so," the Vicar nodded. "You'll be amazed by the simplicity and elegance of my plan. Oh look, he's out! Well bowled, that man! Well bowled!"

THIRTEEN

"Are you absolutely sure about this?" Ogden said.

"Of course I'm sure," the Vicar replied. "In fact, it's one of the few areas where I can be one hundred per cent certain."

He took another sip of his tea and smiled benevolently.

"I did enjoy that cricket match," he added. "You should have joined us, Sybil. They had a demon bowler who reminded me of old Tubby Beeston in 'F' Directorate: you know, those innocuous run-ups, followed by the most devastating—"

"Godfrey, I don't like this," Sybil broke in. "It's dangerous."

"Nonsense," chuckled the Vicar. "Safe as houses."

"It's illegal," Sybil said. "You could go to prison."

"Well, it's funny you should say that. Legally speaking, it's a very grey area. You see, if the phone-tap is unlawful—and it almost certainly is—I doubt if we'd be doing anything wrong."

"You can't be sure of that," Sybil persisted. "Godfrey, I beg you not to do this."

Sybil was genuinely worried. Her hands were clasped tightly together, and she sat nervously on the edge of her armchair. Matters were not helped by the expression of cheery complacency on her husband's face. But Sybil was not the only one who had doubts: even Ogden had shed some of his customary schoolboy recklessness. He blew a large purple gum-bubble, burst it, and said, "Look, Vicar, I know you're the expert, and all that—"

"I certainly am," the Vicar agreed.

"But surely every phone-tap is backed up by a warrant signed by the Home Secretary."

"Not true, Clive. Half the taps in this country are illegal, and even when they've been OK'd by the Home Office, the warrant is only produced in the case of police taps. MI5 warrants are never seen by anybody."

"Including the Telecom people?"

"Especially the Telecom people. They do exactly what they're told. All you need is one of these."

He opened his wallet and took out an identity card, which he passed over to Ogden and the others.

"This expired six years ago," the Laird observed.

"I'll cross it out and write in a new date," the Vicar said. "They won't notice."

"But surely the cards are changed every so often to avoid this kind of thing: a new format, different colours—"

"Oh, of course," the Vicar nodded. "I'm sure the new cards don't look anything like this."

"But—but in that case—?"

"Look," the Vicar said heavily, "we aren't dealing with a tap in central London. It's a remote place, staffed by yokels, and all we need to do is casually wave the card at them. Trust me."

"If you say so," Ogden shrugged.

"I do," said the Vicar, and with a mischievous grin, he added, "Really, Clive, I never thought you'd be the one to get cold feet."

Ogden frowned indignantly at the Vicar.

"Now steady on," he said truculently. "There's no question of cold feet here. Just plain common sense."

"Good," said the Vicar. "So it's settled, then?"

"It certainly is," Ogden snapped. "Anyone here dissent?"

"Not me," Beauchamp said.

"Well," the Laird shrugged, "if the Vicar doesn't know about phone-taps, who does? Let's give it a shot. It sounds like fun, anyway."

"Definitely," the Vicar giggled.

Sybil said nothing, and left the room, as the men discussed the fine details of the Vicar's plan. After a few minutes, Ogden was summoned by a call of nature, and he excused himself. Out in the hallway he was accosted by Sybil, who grabbed his sleeve with surprising force.

"This is all your fault," she hissed. "I won't forget it, you know."

"Oh really, Sybil," Ogden said. "It's the Vicar's idea. You heard him."

"Yes, but who started it all? You and your wretched memoirs—why couldn't you leave us all in peace? Why did you have to cause all this trouble?"

She burst into tears and rushed off to the kitchen, leaving Ogden to scratch his head in bewilderment.

"Women," he sighed. "Never could make 'em out."

He blew another gum-bubble, and went upstairs to the lavatory.

The next day, Ogden & Co. drove over to Tooting, and visited a car dealer called Tony Blewitt, who specialised in selling second-hand commercial vehicles. Mr Blewitt was a youngish man with a large beer-belly and a permanent smile. Nothing, it seemed, was a problem for him.

"Used van?" he said. "No problem. Got dozens."

"Preferably ex-British Telecom," the Vicar added.

"No problem," Mr Blewitt beamed. "Take your pick, gen'lmen."

He led them out into his yard, where around twenty yellow light vans stood in various stages of dilapidation.

"Starts at five hundred quid, gen'lmen," Mr Blewitt explained. "The best one's fifteen hundred. All MOT'd—no problem."

The Vicar looked over two or three vans, and finally settled for a rusty old T-registration model.

"How much is this one?" he asked.

"Five-eighty," Mr Blewitt said.

"You're joking, of course," Beauchamp said. "This is over nine years old."

"Very good nick, though," Mr Blewitt countered. "No rust. Well, not much."

"Four hundred," Ogden offered, and he exhaled a pink ball of gum.

"Now you're joking," Mr Blewitt grinned. "I mean to say—"

"You are prepared to negotiate, aren't you?" the Laird said, waving his pipe-stem solemnly.

"Well, yeah," Mr Blewitt said uneasily. "No problem. But I was thinking more like five-fifty."

"A born comedian," Beauchamp said appreciatively. "You should be on the stage."

"Did he say four-fifty?" the Vicar asked.

"Sounded like it," Ogden said.

"Five-thirty," Mr Blewitt offered.

"Slip of the tongue," the Laird suggested. "You meant four-sixty, didn't you?"

"Five-ten," Mr Blewitt said desperately. "I mean to say—"

"You mean to say four-seventy," Beauchamp corrected him.

"Four-ninety," Mr Blewitt shouted. "Four-ninety, and if you don't like it, you can—"

"Four-ninety it is," Ogden nodded.

"Provided you throw in a can of spray paint," the Vicar added.

"Spray paint?" Mr Blewitt repeated. "What do you want that for? The van's just been re-sprayed—"

"It's for my car at home," the Vicar explained. "A nice royal blue, if you have it."

"Yeah, all right," Mr Blewitt sighed.

"Good man," Ogden said, and he patted Mr Blewitt on the back.

"A gentleman," Beauchamp said.

"A scholar," said the Laird.

"A fucking prat," Mr Blewitt said mournfully.

Having paid up, Ogden & Co. returned to the Vicar's home, and hurriedly drove the van into his garage.

"There's no one about," Ogden said, casting a quick glance up the street.

"Glad to hear it," said the Vicar, as he closed the garage door. "They're all frightful gossips around here."

"What happens now?" Beauchamp asked.

"It's quite simple," said the Vicar. "Mr Blewitt hasn't completely re-sprayed the van: he's just painted over the British-Telecom logos on the outside. If you look carefully at the surface, you can still see the raised markings. I'm going to colour them in once more with the spray paint. I'll also add the letter 'R' to the old van code—that will indicate that the van belongs to Telecom's Reserve fleet. The tappers always use Reserve vans, you see—"

"All right, all right," Beauchamp said. "And how long will all this take?"

"Two hours," the Vicar replied. "Then we'll be ready to go."

"Splendid," Ogden said. "While you're doing that, Vicar, I think we shall cadge a pot of tea from your delectable wife."

"By all means. But—er, easy does it, chaps."

"What's that?"

"Sybil's not on form at the moment. Handle with care."

Ogden saluted smartly.

"Message received and understood."

★

69

By nine o'clock that evening, the van was ready, and the Vicar had made the last of his preparations.

"I've phoned the exchange," he said, "and told them two special engineers would be in tonight."

"They bought that?" Ogden said.

"Gladly," the Vicar nodded. "That tends to suggest that they know who we are."

"Implying that they've had a similar visit recently," the Laird reasoned.

"So Mr Blake's probably right," Beauchamp said. "They have fitted a tap to his phone."

"Possibly," the Vicar said. "But we can't be sure. After all, they might have been tapping someone else. No, Clive and I will still have to see for ourselves."

"Are you sure only one of us can come with you?" asked the Laird.

"Positive," said the Vicar. "They normally work in pairs. And besides, I have only two sets of overalls."

He pulled two crumpled Telecom uniforms out of an old carrier-bag.

"Try one on," he said to Ogden.

"This is going to look a bit silly," Ogden observed, and he was right: the sleeves stopped just below his elbow.

"Roll them up," the Laird suggested.

"Why don't you forget the idea?" Sybil said desperately. "There's still time. You can phone Mr Blake, and—"

"No, dearest," the Vicar said firmly. "We're going tonight. That's fine, Clive: nobody will notice. I'll just check my tool-kit once more, and we'll be off."

Having satisfied himself that everything was in order, the Vicar led his friends out to the garage.

"If you don't hear from us by tomorrow lunch-time," Ogden said, "send for the cavalry."

"Good luck," Beauchamp said.

"Send us a postcard," the Laird suggested.

The journey was wholly uneventful. At that time of night the traffic was fairly light, and they were out of Greater London within an hour. But the journey through Kent was slow: the Vicar wished to avoid major routes, so most of the trip was spent on narrow B-roads that wound through fields and small villages.

After three hours, they arrived at the Telecom exchange which served Mr Blake's phone. It was a medium-sized building just outside a tiny hamlet near Canterbury.

"Pull up at the front," the Vicar commanded.

"Are you sure?" Ogden said. "Isn't discretion the order of the day?"

"Not at all. The style is brusque and businesslike. Just watch me."

The exchange's night staff consisted of one sleepy individual called Jack, who sat in the office reading a copy of *Penthouse*. He showed the two old men in and offered them a coffee, which they accepted gratefully.

"I was expecting the same blokes who come here last time," Jack said.

"They're on another job," the Vicar explained.

"I was sorry about what happened," Jack said. "I mean, the rules say all visiting staff have to sign the visitors' book."

"All except us," said the Vicar.

"Yeah, but no one told me, did they?"

"What happened?" Ogden said.

"They got a bit stroppy," Jack said ruefully. "Pulled rank on me, shouted, told me I could be nicked for obstructing them—basically, the works."

"Don't worry," the Vicar said. "We're nicer than they are. If you keep out of our way, we won't make trouble."

"Fair enough," Jack nodded, and he gave each of his guests a mug of coffee. "If you don't mind my saying so—"

"Yes?"

"Well, aren't you a bit *old* for this caper? I mean, no offence or anything, but the last blokes were a lot younger than you."

"They're juniors," the Vicar said.

"Oh," Jack said.

"And we're seniors," Ogden added.

"I—I see."

"Anyway," said the Vicar. "Enough chit-chat. We've a job to do."

"Yeah," Jack said. "Well, it's this way."

He led them into the exchange, and explained its layout. Then he returned to his office.

"What now?" Ogden asked.

"Let me explain," said the Vicar.

He pointed to one of several large pairs of racks, about ten feet high by thirteen feet wide, which stood face to face and were covered with arrays of electrical contacts.

"Each of these is called a distribution frame. The lines come in from the clients' phones and are fitted to the rear rack in street order. That's called the 'line side' of the frame. The front rack is called the 'exchange side': its contacts are all in number sequence."

"The clients' phone numbers?"

"Precisely. The two frames are linked by all those multi-coloured wires, which are called 'jumpers'. The jumpers cross-connect each incoming line to the appropriate number on the exchange side. This is the last point on the phone circuit where a client's phone can be separated from all the others."

"And therefore the last point at which a phone can be tapped?"

"Correct. So all we have to do is find Mr Blake's number, and look at the circuit."

He looked at his note-pad, and found the number, which he then located on the frame.

"Here we are. Now, what usually happens is that the tap consists of a wire on the line side, which is disguised as one of the ordinary jumpers. This phoney jumper is fitted to something called a 'junction' here on the exchange side. The junction is a connection reserved for a spare line leading to the main telephone network. But this junction doesn't connect with the network: it leads to the nearest Group Switching Centre, and through to the main eavesdropping centre in London."

"Crafty," Ogden nodded.

"And there's no way the staff here could ever spot it."

"In that case, how can you?"

"Simple," the Vicar grinned. "Back here on the line side, each connection has its own fuse—a standard safety precaution. But Mr Blake's connection has a red fuse."

"What does that mean?"

"It's a warning to the engineers: do not touch under any circumstances. The red fuse is used with priority numbers: essential services, such as doctors and fire brigades."

"And people who are being tapped?"

72

"Just so. Now our friend Blake is nobody in particular, and he doesn't have a priority number. So this has to be a tap."

"Well done, Vicar!" Ogden exclaimed.

"It's all different in the new digital exchanges," the Vicar added. "The tapping is done by completely separate means, which are impossible to spot. That's why I asked Blake if his exchange had been modernised. We were quite lucky, really."

"I suppose so," Ogden said. "Well, shall we go?"

"Wait a minute," said the Vicar. "Now we know that Blake really is being tapped, are we going to pursue the matter?"

"I don't know," Ogden shrugged. "Hadn't we better discuss that at home?"

"Yes, but it just occurred to me that if we're going to have further dealings with Blake, we could do him and ourselves a big favour."

"What's that?"

"Take the tap off his phone."

Ogden's face erupted into a broad grin.

"What a lovely idea," he said. "But the tappers will know about it at once when their line goes dead, won't they?"

"Oh, I wasn't proposing to disconnect the tapping circuit," the Vicar said. "Just move it elsewhere."

With some effort, Ogden managed to stop himself laughing out loud.

"Brilliant," he giggled. "Absolutely inspired."

"I thought you'd approve," the Vicar nodded. "Well, here goes."

He opened his tool-kit and went to work on the frame. Twenty minutes later, he had transferred the tap from Blake's line to another one on a nearby distribution frame.

"Heaven knows whose line it is," the Vicar shrugged. "But I bet the boys in London will take weeks to realise what's happened. Very well, let's go home."

They went to the office and said goodnight to Jack.

"All in order," the Vicar said briskly. "And don't forget, we were never here."

"Right you are," Jack said, giving them a broad wink. "I haven't seen a thing."

"Good man," Ogden said.

They left the exchange, and returned to the van. Three hours later, Ogden and the Vicar were back in London.

73

FOURTEEN

Two days later, when Ogden & Co. had caught up on their lost sleep, they met Mr Blake on Wandsworth Common once again. There were no cricketers out today, and the only people around were two or three young mothers with prams. The weather had turned gloomy once more, which seemed to suit Mr Blake's melancholy mood: not surprisingly, Blake was scarcely pleased by what Ogden & Co. had to tell him.

"It doesn't surprise me, of course. But it's still not very agreeable to learn that you're being spied on by your own authorities."

"I wouldn't be too upset," the Vicar said. "It can happen to the nicest people, you know."

"Are you still interested in helping me?" Blake asked. "Of course, I'll understand perfectly if you say 'no'."

"On the contrary," Ogden said, "we'd be delighted to help. It's a fascinating business—"

"And to be honest," said the Laird, "we've nothing better to do."

"Besides," Beauchamp said, "the first payments for Clive's memoirs have come through, so we can afford to do a spot of travelling."

"Ah yes," Blake said. "The memoirs. I've just been reading a copy someone lent me."

There was a curious glint in Mr Blake's eye, and he gazed steadily at Ogden.

"You've clearly had an action-packed life," he observed.

"Oh, indeed," Ogden coughed. "It was all go. Anyway, about your colleague . . ."

"Yes," Blake said. "What do you propose to do?"

"We've talked this through," Ogden said, "and we've decided that each of us will handle a separate strand of the inquiry. The Laird here—I mean, Mr Buchanan—knows something about shipping, and he's going to try and track down the elusive SS

74

Flavio and its captain. Mr Beauchamp is going to look for the equally elusive Dutchman, Lemiers. And I shall go to the United States and find out about Magnum Inc. and the even more elusive Colonel Kyle—after I've had a chat with David Symes."

"That sounds excellent," Blake said gratefully. "I can try to cover most of your expenses—"

"Forget it," said the Laird. "As we've said, we've just been paid something for the memoirs."

"And I have to go to the United States anyway," Ogden added. "There's a Mr Cyrus X. Stompfweiner III in Baltimore who's simply dying to meet me."

"If only he knew," Beauchamp grinned.

"And there are a number of television stations who seem very eager for me to appear on their programmes."

"Don't let it go to your head," the Vicar advised.

"I'll do my best," Ogden said gravely.

"Tell me," Blake said. "Did you—did you really jump out of an aeroplane without a parachute?"

"Eh?" Ogden said. "Well . . ."

The friends glanced at each other, and made a silent decision.

"It was either that," Beauchamp said, "or be cut to pieces by Akhmatov's mad axeman."

"A terrible choice," the Laird sympathised.

"And if you think *that* was bad," the Vicar said, "you should read the next instalment. Something about being lowered head-first into a vat of sulphuric acid."

"While bound in a strait-jacket," Ogden added. "Real Perils of Pauline stuff."

Mr Blake shifted uncomfortably.

"I see," he murmured. "It does all sound rather incredible."

"That," Ogden explained, "is because it's all tripe. One hundred per cent piffle. But it's a living, isn't it?"

FIFTEEN

Brigadier David Symes was one of those lucky people who are virtually unscathed by middle age. He was in his early fifties, but his face was scarcely lined, and his physique had remained unchanged in over thirty years. His hair had turned completely white, but paradoxically this only reinforced his youthful appearance. Sitting next to Ogden in the Special Forces Club, he could easily have passed for the old man's son.

"Delighted to see you, Clive," he said, taking a sip of his Scotch and soda. "I'm sorry I didn't reply to your message sooner, but I've been out of the country for the last few weeks. In fact, I only returned yesterday afternoon, and found your letter under a pile of other stuff."

"Not to worry," Ogden said, waving his hand. "It wasn't screamingly urgent. I've been rather busy myself, with the memoirs and all the attendant nonsense."

"Ah yes," Symes nodded. "I had heard something about your autobiography. Everyone's doing it now, aren't they? I'm surprised you're still in the country."

"Why?"

"Well, aren't they prosecuting you?"

"No," Ogden said. "At least, not to my knowledge."

"But I thought that was their policy?"

"So did I," Ogden shrugged. "Perhaps they've changed their minds. I take it you haven't read any of it?"

"Not yet," Symes admitted. "In fact, I know next to nothing about it. I've been up to my eyeballs in work, you see . . ."

"Of course, of course," Ogden said sympathetically. "Anyway, you'll be relieved to hear that you're not mentioned."

"Fine," Symes grinned. "Who is?"

"Er . . . nobody, actually. At least, nobody is mentioned by their true name."

"That's sensible," Symes observed. "Perhaps it's why you aren't being prosecuted."

76

"Possibly. Who knows? Anyway, you must be wondering why I wanted to see you."

"I was curious."

"It's on behalf of a friend of mine," Ogden said. "He's trying to track down some American chappie in the arms trade. I remembered you were in that line of country, so I thought I'd see if you knew him."

"What's his name?"

"Kyle, Brutus Kyle. Apparently he's a former Marine colonel, or something of the sort. Do you know him?"

"Vaguely," Symes said. "He's put some business my way once or twice. But I know why your friend is having trouble finding him."

"Really?"

"Kyle's gone AWOL. His company ceased trading recently, and the man seems to have gone to ground."

"Any idea why?"

"I'm not sure," Symes said. "He organised a deal recently that went badly wrong. Funnily enough, I was involved in that. You see, I found him a supplier for a medium-sized order. Later, I heard that the deal had blown up, and Kyle had lost a packet. I'd have thought his cash-flow situation would have been good enough to take the strain, but perhaps it wasn't. You only need one or two such disasters to go bust."

"Indeed," Ogden nodded. "So Colonel Kyle could now be sweeping out elephant's cages in some zoo?"

"Quite possibly," Symes grinned. "Though there was another rumour . . ."

"Yes?"

Symes frowned uneasily.

"I stress it's just a rumour. You see, Kyle's a funny chap. A very . . . single-minded fellow. No sense of humour that I could ever discern. He's capable of the worst sort of dewy-eyed sentimentality, but he never smiles."

"Sounds just my type," Ogden said.

"But he was a fine soldier, by all accounts," Symes added hastily. "Purple Heart, and all the rest of it. But—well, the fellow lacks proportion."

"So what's the rumour?"

Symes shook his head sadly.

"Apparently, he's got God in a big way. Oh, I've nothing against the Bible squad, you understand, provided they don't get in people's way. Nothing wrong with the occasional spot of religion—"

"Provided it's occasional and comes in spots," Ogden agreed.

"Exactly," Symes nodded. "That's why I'm a C of E man. But the Americans do it rather differently, I'm afraid. They make a great palaver out it, don't they? Big razzmatazz."

"Hollywood has a lot to answer for," Ogden observed.

"Yes. All this 'born again' business. People taking headers into the blood of Christ. Pretty hysterical, don't you think?"

"And Colonel Kyle has been reborn?"

"So I hear. As a matter of fact, it's been suggested that the colonel's conversion has less to do with God than with an old skull injury he picked up during the Tet offensive. Apparently there's still a fair amount of shrapnel floating around Kyle's bonce."

"Oh dear," Ogden said. "So if Kyle isn't sweeping out elephant's cages, he could well be a fundamentalist preacher."

"Right," Symes said. "But whatever the truth is—yes?"

The Brigadier was interrupted by a discreet tap on the shoulder from one of the club staff.

"Telephone, sir."

"Okay," Symes nodded. "Back in a jiff, Clive."

While the brigadier was taking his call, Ogden reflected on the relevance of Colonel Kyle to the investigation. If Kyle's company had been bankrupted by the disappearance of SS *Flavio*, it meant that Kyle was merely another victim of the swindle, and would have no useful information to offer. And the colonel's sudden attack of religious zealotry had even less bearing on the subject. It seemed that Colonel Kyle and Magnum Inc. of Denver would not offer a fruitful line of inquiry.

When Brigadier Symes returned, there was a troubled expression on his face.

"This is all very embarrassing," he said. "Did you know that you've been blacklisted, Clive?"

"Really?" Ogden said innocently. "By whom?"

"Er, just about everybody, it seems. Sorry about this, but—well, you're now classed as a security risk."

78

"My God," Ogden breathed, trying very hard to look surprised. "When did it happen?"

"No idea," Symes said, "but I think it's something to do with your memoirs. You're not very popular, apparently."

"That's outrageous," Ogden snorted.

"I suppose it is," Symes said unhappily. "I'm most dreadfully sorry, old man. It's very awkward for me, you know. What we've just been talking about—"

"Classified?"

"Absolutely. I don't know why, but Kyle's a bit of a touchy issue at the moment. I'm not supposed to . . . dear oh dear."

"Don't worry," Ogden said soothingly. "We never discussed it."

Symes gazed at him anxiously.

"You're sure about that?"

"Mum's the word," Ogden insisted. "Shan't tell a soul."

Symes' face melted into a relieved grin.

"That's very sporting of you, Clive. I'm much obliged."

Ogden smiled benevolently.

"Anything for a pal," he said.

SIXTEEN

The D-G ran a distressed hand through his hair.

"Ogden again," he complained. "That man is impossible. What exactly happened?"

"Someone spotted the two of them talking in the Special Forces Club," Stringer said. "He checked with us, and we got straight onto Symes. No damage done, as far as I can tell."

"What did Ogden want?"

"He was asking about Kyle, the American."

There was a long silence.

"And that's all?" the D-G asked.

"So Symes says. And he insists he's been discreet. But I still don't like it."

"Quite," the D-G agreed. "I've had my bellyful of Ogden, I really have."

He picked up the latest edition of the *Baltimore Bugle*, and read out the headline in disgust.

"'Philby: the Akhmatov Connection'."

"Oh no," Stringer groaned.

"Oh yes. 'After all these years, the truth can now be revealed. The mysterious agent who recruited Kim Philby to communism and controlled his activities was none other than Yevgeny Akhmatov . . . "I warned them about Philby for years," Ogden says, "but they wouldn't listen."'"

"Bollocks," Stringer observed.

"What can we do?" the D-G said. "Denying this rubbish doesn't seem to work. They think we're just covering up. And I take it you're having no luck."

"None," Stringer admitted. "We've tried virtually everything: we've checked Ogden's bank accounts and those of his mates, going back thirty years. Clean as a whistle. Beauchamp ran an antique business, so we thought we'd find some dirt there. Can you believe it? Beauchamp must be the only honest dealer in the

80

whole history of the antiques trade. He didn't make a penny out of it. And the others are no better."

"Never mind," said the D-G. "Keep trying. You never know what might turn up."

"It's the wrong approach," Stringer said. "We should be getting tough with these people. And it's time the Government changed its policy on memoirs."

"In what way?"

"If the Prime Minister stood up and categorically rejected this bullshit, the problem would disappear."

The D-G shook his head.

"I rather doubt it," he said. "You see, it's too late for that. The papers will still scream 'lies' and 'cover-up', and there'll be even more egg on the PM's face."

"Maybe," Stringer conceded. "But this business with Symes bothers me. Someone's got to tell Ogden to piss off out of it."

"In theory, you're right," the D-G said. "But wouldn't it just encourage him to do it again? You know what he's like."

"True," Stringer said. "But people like Ogden should be dissuaded from approaching former colleagues. Firmly dissuaded."

The D-G smiled wryly.

"You're still dying to break his legs, aren't you?"

"I hate the old bastard," Stringer said savagely. "He's an arrogant, self-satisfied dick-head. Thinks he can do what the fuck he likes."

"With some justification," the D-G admitted.

Stringer brought his fist down onto the D-G's desk.

"God Almighty! I bet he's pissing himself laughing at us. What I'd give to take that fucking bubble-gum of his and make him choke on it."

"Not now," the D-G said firmly. "But your time may come. These memoirs are bound to die down: even Ogden must run out of ideas at some point. And when he does, you may have your chance."

"I'm looking forward to it," Stringer said grimly.

The D-G was struck by a pious afterthought.

"Of course," he said, "there would be no question of taking revenge. This would be entirely a matter of what's best for the security services."

"Oh, naturally," Stringer agreed.

"Ogden would serve as an example."

"Exactly."

"*Pour encourager les autres.*"

"Right."

"Good," said the D-G. "I'm glad that's established. Now, when the fuss does die down, what sort of thing will you have in mind?"

SEVENTEEN

Ogden had been to United States before, but only on business. His brief visits had been confined to the British Embassy in Washington, and such organisations as the CIA and NSA. This was his first opportunity to "have a good long dekko", as he put it, and he intended to make the most of it.

He flew to Baltimore, where Mr Stompfweiner was waiting to greet him. If it were possible, the newspaper proprietor was an even bigger admirer of Ogden than when he had first spoken to him: the mounting extravagance of Ogden's memoirs only served to fan the flames of Mr Stompfweiner's adulation.

Ogden was installed in a luxury hotel in Pleasant Street, where he was given the kind of reception normally reserved for visiting royalty. Each of the rooms in his suite was marginally smaller than the average banqueting hall, and was furnished in the most preposterous "olde worlde" style, with an excess of mahogany panelling, brass fittings, and so forth. Ogden loved every bit of it.

For the first few days, most of Ogden's time was spent meeting local dignitaries at dinners organised by Mr Stompfweiner and his associates, where he was invariably introduced as "Clive Ogden, Superspy". Unlike Britain, where Ogden and his friends were regarded as troublesome old reprobates, the citizens of Baltimore thought Ogden was a tremendous hero, and they queued up to shake his hand and wish him well.

Indeed, the contrast between Ogden's standing here and in Britain did not go unnoticed by his new acquaintances. After assuring Ogden that she was his "number one lifelong fan", one woman asked, "Why do they hate you so much in England? I mean, they ought to give you a medal or something. Why don't they want you to talk about what you've done?"

Ogden nodded thoughtfully, blew a large orange gum-bubble, and popped it.

"A good question, old girl," he said, "and I'm not sure I can answer it. You see, we British are an odd crew. We insist on understating things, and we detest people who boast about their accomplishments. I suspect my memoirs are regarded as a piece of gross immodesty."

"Are you kidding?" the woman said. "You gotta have heroes, Mr Ogden. And you're a hero, right? I mean, what kind of a country doesn't have heroes?"

"Oh, we do have them," Ogden said. "It's just that we prefer them to be dead. Like Nelson and Drake."

The woman thought about it, and shook her head.

"No," she said. "I never heard of them. Anyway, tell me about the time you got cornered by ten Russians in an ice rink, and they came at you with flame-throwers . . ."

Apart from society functions, Ogden was booked in for a series of television interviews. To everyone's amazement, Ogden performed before the cameras like a man born to the task. The producers were a trifle upset by his habit of blowing bubble-gum in the middle of interviews, but no one else seemed to mind. Most importantly, he handled his questioners with skill and confidence. One lady on breakfast television had doubts about Ogden's truthfulness, and she expressed them in a most aggressive manner.

"Suppose I say you're an out-and-out liar?" she suggested.

"Suppose I say you're a beautiful woman," Ogden replied cheerfully. "Then we'd both be talking rot, wouldn't we?"

"But Clive, are you seriously asking me to believe that you staged all these amazing feats of espionage, slept with all these beautiful women, and took on half the KGB single-handed?"

"Not at all. I had two or three colleagues."

"Look, Clive," the woman insisted, "a lot of people have written about the Cold War. How come nobody mentions you?"

"I agree," Ogden nodded. "It's an absurd omission. That's why I wrote the memoirs."

"Sure," she said drily. "Now, what about this guy Akhmatov. Nobody's ever heard of him before, have they?"

"I have," Ogden said.

"The Russians haven't said anything about him, though."

"Have you asked them?"

"Well no," she admitted, "but—"

84

"I think you should. I'd be jolly interested to hear their response."

The interviewer shook her head, and with mounting annoyance, she said, "Gimme a break, Clive. Why don't you admit you're lying through your teeth?"

"That would be impossible," Ogden said, and with a deft manoeuvre he plucked his dentures out of his mouth. "You shee, I don't have any."

The next stop on Ogden's itinerary was New York, where he met the publisher who proposed to issue his collected memoirs in book form. Since the autobiography was guaranteed of instant success, Ogden was given the sort of reception that would make most writers howl with envy: sumptuous dinners were lavished upon him, and within days he was almost a stone heavier.

Amidst all this social whirl, Ogden found time to visit an old friend from his Intelligence days. Chester Peacock was an effete old gentleman who lived with over thirty Persian cats in a rambling apartment building in Greenwich Village. Some twenty years before, he had worked for the CIA in London, where he first made Ogden's acquaintance.

"Clive, darling," Peacock exclaimed, as he showed Ogden into his apartment. "What a delicious surprise!"

"Good to see you, Chester," Ogden smiled, as five or six cats clustered around his feet. "How's things?"

"Oh, fine, fine. *Love* the memoirs, Clive."

"Thank you."

"What I keep asking myself," Peacock said, "is how *does* he get away with it? It's all so *outrageous*."

"Amazing, isn't it?" Ogden chuckled. "Somebody gave me a quote from Julius Caesar: *id quod volunt, credunt.*"

"'They believe what they want to believe'," Peacock nodded. "I guess so. And if you're going to tell lies . . ."

"Tell big 'uns," Ogden grinned.

"Right. I can't get *over* some of these stories: every cliffhanging cliché that's ever been devised—"

"And a few more besides."

"And you even got a death ray in there. A death ray! I mean to *say*! Even the novelists gave up on that gimmick thirty years ago. Well, it all goes to show: there are lies, damned lies, and the memoirs of British Intelligence agents."

"Absolutely," Ogden agreed. "Tell me Chester, are you still in touch with anyone in the Company?"

"Oh sure," Chester said. "I still do some occasional chores for them. There's a *very* nice man in the Latin American section who sometimes—why do you ask?"

"I wondered if you could do a little snooping for me. Nothing too strenuous, of course . . ."

"Sounds *highly* intriguing," Peacock said. "What is it?"

"I'm interested in a fellow called Brutus Kyle. He's an ex-Marine colonel who runs an arms company called Magnum Inc. over in Denver. At least, he did run it: I'm told he's wound up the business and disappeared."

"Yeah? What do you want to know about him?"

"Everything you can get," Ogden said. "I'm going to Denver myself in a couple of days to see if anyone there can tell me anything, but I doubt if I'll have much luck. Apparently Colonel Kyle has done a bedouin impersonation: packed up his tent and vanished in the night."

"Why are you so interested?"

Ogden recounted the story of the missing arms-shipment, and the subsequent murders.

"I don't suppose Kyle would be of much use," Ogden said, "but we're trying every possible lead, and since I'm visiting the States . . ."

"Sure," Peacock nodded. "What a *bizarre* little tale. Almost as *outlandish* as one of your newspaper fictions."

"Can you help?"

Peacock sat back in his armchair and stroked one of the cats, which had settled on his lap. After a pause, he said, "Okay, Clive. Leave it with me. What are you doing over the next couple of days?"

"As I said, I'm flying to Denver. Then I'm off to San Francisco and Los Angeles to meet some more people about the memoirs."

"Busy busy busy."

"Oh, I find time for amusement," Ogden smiled. "I had a splendid time in Baltimore: they've got something called the National Aquarium, which I thoroughly recommend. A bloody great fish tank packed full of sharks and things. Great fun."

"Where are you going after California?"

"Home, theoretically. But I could stop by here, if you'd gathered any information by then."

"I don't see why not," Peacock said. "It shouldn't take me too long to find out about this Kyle person."

"Good show. After I've finished in Denver, I should be back from California in ten days. How does that sound?"

"Fine," Peacock said. "Come back earlier, if you get bored."

"No chance of that," Ogden smiled. "I expect to have a jolly good time in San Francisco. But the one I'm really looking forward to is LA."

Peacock gave a noncommittal shrug.

"Nice, I guess. If you like Californians."

"Oh, to blazes with the Californians," Ogden said. "I want to see Disneyland."

EIGHTEEN

"Anything turned up?" Beauchamp inquired.

"*Niet, Tovarisch,*" said the Laird.

"Ditto," Beauchamp sighed. "This gumshoe lark's a jolly sight harder than it looks."

They were working from Beauchamp's home in Surrey, firstly because Sybil had become fed up with Laird's malodorous pipe-smoke, and secondly because Beauchamp possessed two phone lines, which were a legacy from his defunct antique business. The two men could therefore pursue their separate inquiries from the same address, and pool ideas whenever necessary. At the moment, neither of them was in good spirits.

"I've tried just about everybody," the Laird said. "Each is as useless as the next. The people at Lloyd's register said they haven't a bloody clue where the SS *Flavio* could be, and they wouldn't know how to find out. Pea-brained fools. But everyone else has said more or less the same thing."

"What now?"

"God knows. I suppose if I phone every harbourmaster on the Mediterranean, I must find who's come across the wretched tub. But that could take months."

"Well, you could start with the Italian ports," Beauchamp suggested. "There can't be too many of those. And the *Flavio* does operate from Italy, so it's bound to return there sooner or later."

"Good thinking," the Laird said. "Unfortunately, my Italian isn't up to much."

"So what? English is supposed to be the international language, isn't it?"

"True," the Laird said reluctantly, "but . . . well, we don't rule the waves any more, do we?"

"Can't hurt to try."

"No. I'll do that, then. How about you?"

"I'm floundering," Beauchamp admitted. "In the last two

88

days, I must have spoken to a hundred different arms dealers. Not one of them has ever heard of a Dutchman called Pieter Lemiers."

The Laird pensively scratched one of his sideboards.

"Wrong tack," he said. "You're going over well-trodden ground. That investigator, what was his name—Hopkins, did the same as you, and found nothing. Whoever Lemiers is, I don't think he's an arms trader."

"But he managed to persuade Carter that he was."

The Laird shrugged.

"The other night, the Vicar managed to persuade someone that he was a Telecom engineer. He bloody well isn't, though."

"Point taken," Beauchamp said. "But what are we left with? Lemiers is Dutch, and he knows about shipping things. That narrows down the field to about five million people."

"He also knows about forged end-user certificates. There can't be too many Dutch people in that position."

"Fair enough," Beauchamp said, "but if he's not in the arms business—"

"Let's just say he knows about shipping things illegally. Now, if the man's a criminal, he may have a record."

"That's a thought," Beauchamp said. "How would we find out?"

"Haven't the foggiest," the Laird smiled. "I just get the ideas. It's up to you peasants to make 'em work."

"Very well," Beauchamp said. "I'll think it over."

The Laird went back to his telephone to begin phoning the Italian ports, and Beauchamp spent the next half hour in silent contemplation. Perhaps, he thought, an old Intelligence contact might help. It seemed unlikely: he'd never had dealings with Dutch Intelligence, and he knew nobody who had. Furthermore, this was a criminal matter, which was wholly outside Beauchamp's experience. Just as he was about to write the idea off altogether, something occurred to him.

Beauchamp did know a policeman—a Superintendent Day of the Fraud Squad, whose acquaintance he had made during his time in the antiques trade. Beauchamp had been offered a large number of Victorian bronze figurines at knock-down prices. He recognised them as forgeries, and refused the offer, but other dealers were less fortunate. Superintendent Day led the investigation, and interviewed Beauchamp in the course of inquiries. The two men got on quite well, and Day later became one of Beauchamp's regular clients. Perhaps he was worth a try.

Beauchamp looked inside his wallet and found Day's card. Three minutes later, the two men were speaking over the phone.

"This is a pleasant surprise, Jeremy," Day said. "I thought you'd retired with your millions."

"Well, you're half right," Beauchamp smiled. "I am retired. And this is nothing to do with antiques, actually."

"No?"

"No. I was wondering if I could ask a favour of you . . ."

Beauchamp explained that he was trying to trace a Dutchman called Pieter Lemiers on behalf of a friend, but was having no luck.

"There's a possibility that Lemiers has a criminal record. If so, the Dutch police might know his present whereabouts."

Beauchamp could hear a heavy intake of breath at the other end of the line.

"Is this something I should know about, Jeremy?"

"Not at all," Beauchamp said. "I don't think Lemiers has committed any crimes recently."

"If you say so, old son. But this is a tall order, you know."

"Is it?"

"I'm not supposed to give you the contents of our records, never mind those of the Dutch."

"I suppose not," Beauchamp said. "In that case, I'm sorry to have bothered you—"

"Wait a minute, wait a minute. I didn't say I was helpless. What do you know about this guy Lemiers?"

"Nothing, beyond what I've told you. He was in Paris on the dates I mentioned, and since then he's disappeared."

"Okay," Day said. "Leave it with me. I'm not promising anything, mind."

"Of course not."

"I'll get back to you tomorrow, all right?"

"Fine," Beauchamp said. "Many thanks."

He put the phone down, and looked up to see the Laird grinning from sideboard to sideboard.

"Eureka," the Laird said, triumphantly waving his pipe.

90

"Found the *Flavio*?"

"On my fourth attempt. It's in the port of Livorno—Leghorn, to you—and it's due to leave in two days."

"Congratulations," Beauchamp said. "What now?"

The Laird thought about it, and said, "I suppose I'd better go there, hadn't I?"

NINETEEN

Mr Blake's phone was tapped according to a well-established system. Whenever his line was in use, the voices would automatically set off a tape recorder in the tapping centre. The tapes would be transcribed by one of the typists and sent off to the 'client' in MI5. At the same time, two gentlemen called Wayne and Kevin took turns to listen to the phone calls as they occurred, on the off-chance that something might be said which would require an immediate response from the client.

Wayne and Kevin found most of Mr Blake's calls boring. In fact, they found most people's calls boring, but Mr Blake's were exceptionally dull. Mr Blake spoke in the kind of dense, gloomy voice that could make the most incorrigible optimist dial for the Samaritans. Furthermore, most of his calls were to and from the medical authorities, and it was clear that Mr Blake was far from well. Wayne and Kevin did not know the precise nature of Mr Blake's complaint, but they understood that it required copious amounts of drugs, few of which seemed to do Mr Blake any good. All in all, they found Mr Blake a depressing fellow, and they wished that he would stop paying his phone bills and be disconnected.

At once, however, things began to look up. There was a new voice on Mr Blake's phone, and Wayne and Kevin found it a great improvement. For one thing, the voice was female, and belonged to someone called Sharon. Of course, it was not the eavesdroppers' task to interpret what they heard—that was the client's job—but they could not help speculating on this new development. They supposed that Mr Blake's illness had taken a turn for the worse, and that he was now bedridden and being looked after by a nurse.

It was a reasonable guess, since Mr Blake no longer used his phone, and Sharon was the only one to make outgoing calls from his home. But if Sharon was Mr Blake's nurse, she took her duties very lightly. She spent a great deal of time on Mr Blake's phone, making personal calls. Indeed, her calls were so personal that Wayne and Kevin had no hesitation in describing her as a "goer".

"Never heard nothing like it," Wayne said.

"Oh, I don't know," Kevin said thoughtfully. "There was that bird in the anti-apartheid movement who was shagging half the London School of Economics. And what about that one in Dunstable CND? She was a right goer."

"Fair enough," Wayne conceded. "But have you seen all these numbers she's been phoning? Eighteen of them, for Christ's sake. And they're all married men. Where does she get the time?"

"Where does she get the energy?"

"What a goer," Wayne said, shaking his head. "Look out, she's at it again."

The tape recorder started once more, and the two men hurriedly put on their headphones.

"Hello?" Sharon said.

"That you Sharon?"

"Yeah."

"It's me, Stan. You free tonight?"

"No. How about Wednesday?"

"Yeah, all right. It's arrived."

"What has?"

"The rubber gear."

"Yeah?"

"Can't wait to try it. Have you got the jelly?"

"Yeah. Should be fun."

"Wednesday then."

"See you."

"Bye."

"My God," Kevin said, as he peeled off his earphones. "Did you hear that?"

"Amazing," Wayne said. "What a goer."

"At Blake's house! He's going to see her there. By Christ, that Blake must be a sick man."

"Death's door," Wayne agreed. "Can you imagine it? Him upstairs dying in his bed, and down below she's having a rubber party."

Kevin consulted his notes, and found more cause for astonishment.

"Stan's new," he breathed. "We've not had him before. So he's . . ."

"Number nineteen!" Wayne exclaimed.

For a full minute they sat in awed silence, trying to comprehend the sheer athleticism of Sharon's social life.

"She must be bow-legged," Kevin concluded.

"Good thing she's using jelly," Wayne said. "Otherwise there wouldn't be much of her left."

Kevin nodded slowly.

"What a goer," he said.

TWENTY

Chester Peacock trembled with excitement, as he gave Ogden a thick sheaf of notes.

"Clive," he said, "you'll just *love* all this. I promise."

"You found out something, then?"

"Did I find out something! Clive darling, Magnum Inc. of Denver was a CIA-front company."

Ogden's eyebrows lifted inquiringly, and he expelled a vermilion gum-bubble.

"Start at the beginning," he suggested.

"Well, I first approached this man I know who works in Signals Interception. He'd heard about Kyle—I could tell—but he wasn't going to give me *anything*. In fact, he got all hoity-toity with me and said it was none of my damn business. I said, 'All right, all *right*. You aren't putting any boils on *my* ass. I'll just try somewhere else.'"

"Good for you," Ogden grinned.

"And I did. A *very* nice girl in the Far-Eastern section knew all about Magnum. Apparently it was one of a number of front companies the CIA use to sell arms in secret."

"To whom?"

"Anyone they like. But I understand that Kyle's speciality was central and southern America."

"So the arms he bought from Carter were probably destined for the Nicaraguan Contras?"

"Or Panama, or somewhere like that."

"And the CIA was bankrolling this operation?"

"So I'm told," Peacock nodded.

"In that case," Ogden said, "one of our theories has just gone down the plug-hole."

"What's that?"

"Magnum Inc. didn't close through bankruptcy. However much Kyle lost on the theft of Carter's shipment, his people could afford it."

"You're right," Peacock said. "And nobody really understands why Kyle stopped trading. Apparently he just walked into the office one day and told all his staff to go home."

"Any theories?"

"No *good* ones. There's some talk that Kyle got religion—but hell, half of the armed forces are born-again Christians now. It never stopped anyone from fighting, did it?"

"Not in my experience," Ogden smiled.

"Anyway, I got a copy of his file. Thought you'd like it."

"You bet," Ogden said appreciatively. "Chester, you've done splendidly."

"*De rien*," Peacock shrugged modestly.

"You've certainly outgunned me," Ogden said. "Denver was a total waste of time. I went to Magnum Inc.'s offices, and found they were completely empty. The commissionaire told me Colonel Kyle was a very agreeable fellow who always asked after his wife, and no, he didn't know what had become of him. There wasn't even a forwarding address."

"Doesn't surprise me," Peacock said. "Kyle sounds like a real zero, and I don't think you'll find his résumé very useful. He's really *very* boring: decorated Vietnam veteran, and all that usual crud."

"Any personality quirks?"

"None listed. He's conscientious, efficient, clean-living, blah blah blah. There's a wife and kids somewhere. There *would* be, of course."

Ogden glanced through the file, and nodded in resignation.

"End of lead," he concluded. "Kyle isn't going to get us anywhere, from the look of this. But there's still one small question mark."

"Yes?"

"Kyle was put in touch with Carter by a British officer called Symes, who has Intelligence connections. Hitherto, I've assumed that Kyle knew Symes via the gun trade. But it's now just possible that they were Intelligence colleagues."

"True," Peacock said. "But so what?"

"Our Intelligence people have been tapping the phone of Carter's business partner, and they seem to be taking a keen interest in his activities. We can't understand why. But if Carter's arms shipment was an Intelligence operation that went wrong—"

"An *illegal* operation," Peacock said.

"There would have been quite a few red faces when it was learned that a massive outfit like the CIA had been swindled by some grubby Italian sea captain."

"Definitely. So you think there's been a cover-up?"

"Seems plausible," Ogden said. "Though it doesn't explain Carter's murder, or that of the private investigator."

"Maybe they were killed as part of the cover-up," Peacock suggested.

"I rather doubt it," Ogden said. "What's the point? By all accounts, Carter was having no luck with his inquiry, and the investigator was in a similar position. And killing them just served to draw attention to whatever's being concealed. After all, if it weren't for those killings, we wouldn't be having this conversation, would we?"

"I guess not," Peacock conceded. "Oh well, what are you going to do now?"

"Don't know," Ogden said. "I was sure I had something else to take care of while I was in the States, but it's slipped my mind."

"Must have been trivial," Peacock said.

"Probably," Ogden agreed. "Anyway, that's my work here finished. Time to go home, and see if one of my chums has had better luck."

"I wish you well. It sounds *much* more exciting than those stories you've made up for your memoirs."

"Perhaps," Ogden grinned. "But they're fun as well. Oh, and speaking of fun, I must tell you about Disneyland . . ."

TWENTY-ONE

"Jeremy? It's John Day, here."

"Hello," Beauchamp said. "Any success?"

"Maybe," Day said. "I've found out about a Pieter Lemiers, but I'm not sure if he's your man."

"Why is that?"

"I phoned a liaison officer in the Netherlands police, and he told me I was wasting my time. There were several Lemiers with criminal records, but only one was called Pieter, and he's doing five years for robbery."

"Oh dear."

"He said he'd need more information to trace the guy—an address, occupation, something like that. So I thanked him and rang off."

"Never mind," Beauchamp said, "it was good of you to—"

"He phoned me back two hours later," Day continued. "Apparently he'd chatted about my call to his mates, and one of them remembered the name from somewhere else."

"Really?"

"He checked the files, and lo and behold: a Pieter Lemiers was murdered two months ago in Rotterdam."

"Good heavens!"

"Shot dead in his office, apparently. The case is still under investigation, but the word is that there are no clues, no suspects, and no apparent motive for the killing."

Beauchamp picked up a note-pad and began scribbling upon it.

"What was Lemiers' occupation?"

"He ran a chemical supply company called Leipochem. He travelled around a lot, so he could have been in Paris on the dates you gave me. Do you think he's your man?"

"To be quite honest, I've no idea. I wasn't expecting him to be a chemical supplier—but then, I wasn't expecting him to be anything, I suppose."

"There's a widow, if you're interested."

"I am," Beauchamp said. "Do you have her address?"

"Sure," Day said. "She lives in Rijswijk. That's a suburb of the Hague, apparently."

Beauchamp wrote down both Mrs Lemiers' address and that of Lemiers' company.

"That's all I could get," Day concluded. "Hope it's what you want."

"I hope so too," Beauchamp said. "I'm deeply grateful—"

"No sweat," Day laughed. "But I tell you what: if you come across any nice bits of Regency furniture, give me first shout."

"I'll do that," Beauchamp promised. "Thanks again."

"Cheers."

Beauchamp put the phone down, and rushed out to his car. An hour later, he was at the Vicar's home, recounting the latest news.

"What do you think?" he said finally.

"I really don't know," said the Vicar, scratching his head. "He could be our Lemiers, I suppose. But why would a chemical supplier be selling arms? The two activities are hardly related."

"They aren't related at all," Sybil said. "He's the wrong man."

"But he was abroad at the time in question," Beauchamp countered. "It could have been Paris."

"It could also have been Kuala Lumpur," Sybil said. "You don't know."

"I could try to find out. His wife should know, or his colleagues."

"That's right," Sybil said bitterly, "pester some poor widow at the time of her grief. Just what I'd expect—"

"Oh, come on, Sybil," the Vicar said, "we can be tactful, you know."

"I see precious little evidence of that around here," Sybil sniffed.

"Have you any other leads, Jeremy?" the Vicar asked.

"None, I'm afraid. That's why I feel we ought to pursue this one. I admit there's only a slim chance that this is our man—"

"No chance at all," Sybil snorted.

"—but we can't dismiss it."

The Vicar nodded slowly, and said, "What do you suppose Clive would think, if he were here?"

"You know perfectly well, Godfrey," Sybil said. "Clive Ogden can be relied upon to take any course of action that's rash, pointless, thoughtless, childish, and dangerous."

"He'd be over to Holland like a shot," the Vicar agreed.

"In that case, I'd better go," Beauchamp said. "Besides, I could do with a quick holiday."

"Aha," Sybil said accusingly. "Now we're getting to the truth of the matter. You just want a pleasure trip, and any pretext will do."

"Now, wait a minute, Sybil—"

"No, Jeremy Beauchamp, *you* wait a minute. Just because Clive is having a nice time abroad, you all want an excuse to do the same. Let's face it, that's why Fergus has rushed off to Italy. Well, if you want a holiday, why don't you go to an ordinary resort like everyone else? There's no need to take advantage of some poor widow's grief. If I were her, I would send you packing. But I expect she's a kind-hearted, trusting soul who'll take you at your face value. You may not have any respect for people in mourning, but I do. I bet you haven't given the slightest thought to the effect you might have on somebody like that. Why, she might have a nervous breakdown! And whose fault would that be? Yours, and that other irresponsible fool Clive Ogden's. When are you going to come to your senses and stop pretending to be the Famous Five? It's really quite pathetic."

The Vicar stroked his chin thoughtfully and said, "Mmm. I wonder how the Laird is faring in Italy?"

TWENTY-TWO

"Mr Bookana?" said the harbourmaster. "You phone yesterday?"

"That was me," said the Laird. "Is the SS *Flavio* still here?"

"Sure. You go twenty metres that way, turn left, then another fifty metres. Is just there, okay?"

"Thank you."

The Laird left the harbourmaster's office, and followed his directions. The seafront of Livorno was much like any other: weatherbeaten, cluttered with cranes and cables, and smelling of oil and salt. But the town itself was surprisingly pleasant. Livorno was not a tourist paradise, of course, but it was lively and interesting, with enough reminders of its eight-hundred-year history to justify a brief sightseeing tour after the Laird had accomplished his mission.

He stopped in front of a grubby old freighter, lit his pipe, and smiled in satisfaction: through the rust and grime on the ship's stern, he could make out the words "FLAVIO Panama". He looked up at a boy on the deck, and called out: "Captain Salvucci? Ricardo Salvucci?"

The boy made a gesture of understanding, and disappeared inside. Moments later, a man appeared on the top deck and gazed down inquiringly at the Laird.

"*Si?*" he called out.

"Captain Salvucci? I'd like a word, please. It's about a man called Carter."

The man paused, as if trying to decide upon something. Then he shrugged and came down to the quay. The Laird had expected someone older, with a dark complexion, and perhaps a three-day growth of oily black stubble. But the *Flavio*'s captain was not much over thirty, with pale green eyes and hair bleached almost white by the sun. And although the Laird assumed he would be greeted with hostility and evasiveness, Captain Salvucci's expression suggested nothing more than affable bemusement.

"Who are you?" he inquired.

"My name's Buchanan. I'm a friend of Mr Carter's business partner. He's been trying to find you for some time."

"Why?"

"For starters, he'd like to know what you did with a consignment of goods destined for England."

The captain's eyes widened.

"What goods? I never take nothing to England."

"I know you didn't," the Laird said. "That's the whole point. You should have taken a consignment of guns to Southampton, shouldn't you?"

"Guns? *Fucili?*"

"Among other things, yes."

The captain grinned and shook his head.

"You make mistake. I never ship guns anywhere."

"You were supposed to."

"No," the captain said emphatically. "Is no' true. I no' take guns."

"It's all right," the Laird said. "I'm not telling the police anything—"

"You tell the police what you want. The *Flavio* no' take guns."

"But you did meet Mr Carter, didn't you?"

"Oh, sure."

"And he did put a consignment on your ship."

"He watch while we load," the captain said. "But it was no' guns. Other thing."

"What other things?"

The captain waved his hand incredulously, as if the Laird was making an absurd request.

"How do I remember? I done four, five trips since. Maybe fertiliser or something. I forget."

"Fertiliser?" the Laird repeated.

"*Si.* Something like that. You want to know? Follow me."

Captain Salvucci led the Laird onto his ship, and showed him into his cabin. After a few minutes' rifling through a drawer, he unearthed some papers.

"Old cargo manifest and *polizza di carico* are in my office in Napoli," he explained, "but these are Custom and other paper. Look."

The Laird glanced through the cargo documents, and saw nothing except a long list of agricultural commodities—mostly chemical goods, marked down as fertilisers and insecticides, and destined for Greece, Cyprus and Turkey. One of the consignments, which went to the Turkish port of Mersin, was from a "Sig. Carter, Parigi".

"See?" the captain said. "No guns."

"So it says," the Laird nodded. "But as I understood it, the guns were disguised as chemicals and hidden in drums."

The captain seemed to find this idea highly entertaining. He laughed out loud, and took back the papers.

"Big joke, eh? Disguise as chemical? Listen, Signor Bookana, before we leave Napoli, the port police inspect this shipment."

"They did?" the Laird blinked.

"Sure. Is routine, no?"

"And—and they looked at the fertilisers and stuff?"

"Everything."

The Laird was deeply confused. Nothing added up, and if the captain was lying, he was a master of the art.

"Did Mr Carter see these papers?" he asked.

The captain half-closed his eyes in thought, then shook his head.

"No. He just ask to see the *buono di consegna*—how you say, the delivering . . ."

"The delivery note?"

"*Ecco*, the delivery note, from the truck driver."

"So it's possible that Mr Carter didn't know where the goods were going?"

This suggestion took the captain aback.

"But he knew," he said. "He must know . . ."

"Did you tell him?"

"Yes of course. On the telephone."

"You dealt with him by phone before?"

"Always. He phone from Paris, tell me what he want sent where. When he come here, nothing else to talk about."

"You mean, when he came to oversee the loading?"

"Yes. Mr Carter, he just come one afternoon, ask if these thing arrive. I say yes, and show him the delivery note. A very quiet man, Mr Carter—he say almost nothing. Just watch us put them on ship, and he gone."

"And that's all?"

"Sure."

"Did he say anything else? Anything at all? Please think hard."

The captain thought hard, and then he snapped his fingers.

"Yes," he said excitedly. "He say one other thing. Very strange, now I think. He say, 'I wait to meet you at the other end.'"

"Why was that strange?"

The captain shrugged.

"No point. The shipping agent in Turkey, he handle everything there. Why should Mr Carter go there?"

"You assumed that Mr Carter meant that he would be waiting for you in Turkey?"

"Of course. Where else?"

"I think he meant Southampton," the Laird said.

"Southampton? You crazy. I never go to Southampton. Only work in Mediterranean."

"Yes, but did Mr Carter know that?"

The captain laughed.

"Sure. He tell me to send these things to Turkey, remember. On the phone. He must know."

"Of course," the Laird said, but he was far from convinced. "Can you describe Mr Carter to me?"

"Fifty, fifty-five year old. Tall like you, but not so big. Brown hair, short. *Occhiali*—how you say?—glasses."

The Laird nodded. Blake had shown him a photograph of Carter and the description tallied.

"Like I say, he was a very quiet man. No big conversation. *Furtivo* . . ."

"Secretive?"

"*Si.*"

"I think I can explain that," the Laird smiled.

"He think we take guns?"

"Exactly."

The captain laughed heartily, as if the Laird had just recounted a vintage anecdote.

"Very good," he said appreciatively. "I tell my brother this story. Very, very good."

The Laird grinned sheepishly.

"Yes," he admitted, "I suppose it is rather a classic. But tell me, do you know where the goods went after the shipping agent took charge of them at Mersin?"

"One moment," the captain replied, and he took another look through the documentation. "Here: from the agent."

He pointed to a carbon copy of the agent's bill of receipt. Most of the goods were destined for a Turkish company called Egridir Fertilisers; the rest were for the State Organisation for Chemical Industries in Baghdad. The Laird wrote this information down, but he knew he was probably wasting his time.

"Thank you for helping me," he said to the captain. "We still have a mystery on our hands, but I think you've done all you can to solve it."

"Pleasure," the captain smiled. "If you want more information, come to my hotel."

"Where's that?"

"The Hotel San Marino, on the Borgo dei Cappuccini. Is very close to here. But remember, we leave early tomorrow morning."

"I'll bear that in mind," the Laird said. "Thanks again."

"*Arrivederci.*"

The Laird left the *Flavio* and returned to the Via San Giovanni, which led him back into the town centre. He felt deeply confused, and wondered what the others would say when he reported back to them. Clearly, the guns had never been loaded onto the *Flavio*, but had been taken elsewhere. That assumed, of course, that there really had been a consignment of arms. It was quite possible that they never existed. But if so, how could an experienced dealer like Carter have been duped so badly? It didn't make sense.

The Laird sighed ruefully, and decided to put the matter to one side. Since his inquiries had proved fruitless, he would console himself with a few days' gentle sightseeing. He found a newspaper kiosk in the main square, and picked up a copy of the *Daily Telegraph*. Then he sought out a quiet café with an outdoor seat, refilled his pipe bowl, and ordered himself a coffee. If the Laird required any further consolation, he found it on page two of his newspaper, with a headline that said, "Soviet Spy Speaks on TV."

The Laird sat bolt upright in his seat, and coughed out a mouthful of espresso.

"*What?*" he spluttered. "'Yevgeny Akhmatov interviewed on Russian television' . . . that's bloody incredible!"

105

TWENTY-THREE

"Bloody incredible," Stringer said. "Why the fuck have they done it?"

"Why do they do anything?" the D-G replied. "To make trouble, for us, of course."

They were gazing at the newspaper item which had caused the Laird such great mirth. Beneath a blurred photograph of a white-haired old man, the article explained that Yevgeny Akhmatov, the notorious Soviet spy, had been interviewed by Gostelradio, the Russian TV network.

Akhmatov claimed that, after a long and action-packed career, he had retired in 1973 and settled down in an apartment in Semipalatinsk. He confirmed that for many years his arch-enemy had been the British agent Clive Ogden, and that the dramatic events recounted in Ogden's memoirs really had occurred.

Of course, Akhmatov disputed Ogden's version of many episodes, and insisted that he had acquitted himself with distinction. But he was prepared to acknowledge that Ogden was a brilliant agent, and a truly worthy opponent: "If only he'd been working for us", Akhmatov said wistfully.

When asked about the beautiful double-agent, Sylvia von Hubschen, the old man's eyes filled with tears. He said that their love affair had been a beautiful, tempestuous thing, and that the eternal triangle involving himself, Sylvia and Ogden epitomised the complex relationship between East, West and Central Europe.

Finally, Akhmatov was asked if he too was contemplating whether to write his memoirs. He said that originally he had sworn himself to secrecy, and had never intended to trumpet his exploits: those who needed the information already had it, he said. But he admitted that Ogden's memoirs had caused him to think again. After all, he was a good Marxist, and he understood the importance of history. If it became likely that Ogden's version

106

of events would be accepted as historical truth, then Akhmatov would be obliged to set the record straight.

"Cheeky bastards," Stringer said. "I bet they're pissing themselves laughing over this."

"I'm sure they are," the D-G agreed. "But it's no laughing matter. Now everybody believes Ogden's telling the truth."

"Of course they bloody do," Stringer said. He jabbed his finger at the article. "This is all crap, of course, but has anyone checked it? There might be some small scrap of truth here—just enough to let us prosecute Ogden."

"That's what I thought," the D-G said. "I asked Beeching in 'S' Directorate. Apparently there was an Akhmatov at the Soviet Embassy here—"

"Excellent," Stringer said.

"—but he was nobody in particular. A translator, or something. Wasn't even working for the KGB."

"How can Beeching be sure?"

"Some French agent tried to seduce Akhmatov. The Russians found out and sent him home. That's the whole point: Akhmatov was a silly little nobody, and Ogden's made him into an operatic villain. Another example of Ogden's sense of humour."

"I don't know about you," Stringer said through clenched teeth, "but I've had it up to here with Ogden's sense of humour. It's really getting me down."

"You're not the only one," said the D-G. "In forty-five minutes I have an appointment with the PM. I'm not looking forward to it."

"About this?"

"What else? Apparently some MP has tabled a series of questions in the House of Commons, demanding to know if any of it's true. How would you reply?"

"Christ knows. Refuse to comment, I suppose."

"Exactly. It won't look very good, will it? Tantamount to a confirmation."

"But can't the PM drop a hint? Some crack like 'the Russians are deliberately taking advantage of a delicate situation', or something like that?"

The D-G shook his head sadly.

"You'd make a rotten politician, Geoff. If the PM admits that there's a 'delicate situation', half the Commons will want to know why Ogden hasn't been prosecuted for creating the 'delicate situation' in the first place."

"I see," Stringer muttered. "Can of worms, isn't it?"

"And the PM will want to know how we're handling it. What do you suggest I say?"

Stringer spread his hands defensively.

"I'm doing everything I can. We've dug out every file, tapped every phone, grilled every contact. Believe me, the minute I get anything that could put Ogden behind bars, you'll be told."

The D-G looked sceptical.

"How likely is that?"

Stringer looked down at his shoes.

"Not very. Ogden's abroad at the moment, and we've taken the opportunity to look over his home. Nothing there, I'm afraid. A few classified papers, but Ogden's entitled to have them, and none of it's been used in the memoirs."

"Of course it hasn't," the D-G said. "Ogden isn't that stupid. What's he doing abroad?"

"He's in the States, fixing a deal with his publisher. The bastard must be rolling in money by now. According to the CIA, he's been put up in luxury hotels, wined, dined—"

"Is that all he's doing?" the D-G asked sharply. "No more inquiries about Colonel Kyle?"

"None that we know of. He did fly to Denver—"

"Did he indeed?"

"And found nothing. The offices are empty, and nobody there knows anything."

"Let's hope he gives in," the D-G said. "For all our sakes. Now, let's be quite clear about what I'm telling the PM . . ."

TWENTY-FOUR

Captain Ricardo Salvucci returned to his hotel at about nine p.m. Tomorrow would be a busy day, and the captain always took an early night before setting sail.

He lay down on his bed and picked up a paperback novel left behind by the room's previous occupant. It wasn't well-written, and the captain grew bored with it after several pages. He tossed it to one side and lit a cigarette.

The captain couldn't stop thinking about the funny, red-faced old Englishman with the pipe who had visited him this morning. Hilarious. And the expression on his face when told that his consignment of arms was nothing more than a few drums of weed-killer . . .

There was a tap on the door, and the captain glanced up in surprise. His men knew better than to disturb him at this hour, and the same went for the hotel owner, who knew him well. Of course, he *had* given the hotel's address to the Englishman.

"*Si?*" he called out.

The door opened, but it was not the Englishman who came inside. Captain Salvucci had never seen this man before: he would have remembered the crew-cut hair and those peculiar eyes. He peered inquiringly at the man, who whispered in English: "Why hast thou deceived me thus?"

"What?"

"Why hast thou deceived me thus?" the man repeated.

"Who are you?" asked the captain.

The man smiled unpleasantly.

"Ask now of the days that were past, which were before thee."

The captain's command of English was reasonably good, but this form of language was entirely new to him.

"I don' understand," he said, shaking his head. "You in wrong room, maybe?"

The other man shook his head emphatically.

109

"I think so," the captain insisted. "Some kind of mistake, eh? You want someone else."

The man's lip curled contemptuously.

"Thy tongue is like a sharp razor, O worker of treachery," he declared. "Thou lovest evil over good, and lying over truthfulness."

"You crazy," the captain laughed. "I no' lie to you. What you want? Give me a message, maybe?"

The man smiled and nodded.

"A message," he repeated.

"Okay," the captain shrugged. "What is it?"

"The Lord shall smite thee with consumption and with fever, inflammation, and fiery heat, and with drought, and with blasting and with mildew."

The captain was not entirely sure what some of these things were, but he grasped the general idea.

"You definitely crazy," he frowned. "I think we speak to Signor Bianchi downstair. Why he let you in here?"

He stubbed out his cigarette and began to get up from the bed, but the man stepped forward and brought his hand down onto the captain's chest.

"*Pazzo*," the captain breathed.

He tried to get up, but the other man was alarmingly strong. The captain was no weakling himself, and he threw a fierce punch at the man's jaw. It seemed to have no effect, and the other man replied with a blow to the head that nearly rendered the captain unconscious. Several further punches landed on various parts of the captain's anatomy, and left him sagging helplessly on the mattress.

"Behold," the man whispered, "like the clay in the potter's hand, so art thou in my hand."

The captain nodded weakly. There was nothing else to say.

110

TWENTY-FIVE

"Mrs Lemiers? I'm Jeremy Beauchamp. So glad you could find the time to see me. I do hope I'm not . . . disturbing you."

"Not in the least," Mrs Lemiers said calmly.

Beauchamp judged her to be in her middle- to late-forties. She was an attractive woman, with an elegant, cultivated bearing. Her face was grey and lined, and had not been made-up for some time. Her clothes were expensive, but badly crumpled and carelessly thrown on. She looked infinitely weary and indifferent: Beauchamp knew something about grief, and he could tell that this woman was suffering it in its blackest and most soul-rending form.

"When you phoned, you said it was about Pieter," she said, as she showed Beauchamp into her sitting-room, "but you weren't sure. What did you mean by that?"

"Quite simply, I'm not sure if your husband's the man I'm looking for. He probably isn't. I only have the surname Lemiers, and my inquiry concerns something very different from his normal line of work."

"What's that?"

Beauchamp hesitated. He had dreaded this moment ever since he boarded the flight from London. For the entire journey, he had struggled to find a delicate form of words, a decent euphemism for something that would sound terrible, however it was put.

"The man I'm looking for sold military goods to a friend of mine in England."

To Beauchamp's intense relief, Mrs Lemiers showed no reaction.

"You mean he was an arms dealer," she said.

"That's right," Beauchamp nodded. "At least, he did deal in arms on one occasion that I know of."

"To your friend?"

"Yes."

Mrs Lemiers shook her head.

111

"My husband was not an arms dealer," she said simply.

"He never—?"

"Not to my knowledge. Pieter traded in industrial chemicals." There was no hostility in her voice; she was simply stating a fact.

"You're quite sure that's all? There was no side-line, or . . ."

Mrs Lemiers smiled sadly.

"If there was, he never told me."

Beauchamp took a deep breath. He was enjoying this even less than Mrs Lemiers.

"Is it at all possible that he *could* have done something of the kind without your knowledge?"

She shrugged laconically.

"Anything's possible, I suppose. But as I say, he never told me."

"Did he travel abroad?"

"Yes. All over Europe."

"Including Paris?"

"France, certainly. He was also in West Germany, Italy, Switzerland—everywhere. So he might have gone to Paris as well—I just don't know."

And you don't care either, Beauchamp thought. How the hell do I get through to you?

"I'm sorry," she added. "I suppose I'm not being very helpful."

"That's all right," Beauchamp said hastily.

He twiddled his thumbs and glanced around the room. For the first time, he noticed that it contained some very expensive items. There must be a lot of money to be made in the chemicals business, Beauchamp reflected.

"That's a lovely vase," he observed. "Han Dynasty, isn't it?"

Mrs Lemiers' eyes widened slightly.

"You know about these things?"

"Only a little," Beauchamp admitted. "That porcelain dish goes back to the fourteenth century, the Yuan dynasty. It's worth a great deal of money. The glazed figurines—let me see—they're T'ang dynasty, aren't they?"

"That's right," Mrs Lemiers said. "We collected antiques, mainly for investment. But my husband was very fond of Chinese pottery."

"He had excellent taste," Beauchamp said. "I do like that glazed bottle vase—the deep copper-red colour's absolutely marvellous, isn't it? Now that has to be Ch'ien Lung."

"It is," Mrs Lemiers smiled. "You know more than a little about the subject, I think."

"I used to deal in antiques," Beauchamp said. "I wasn't an expert, but I could recognise beautiful things. And these are very beautiful."

Mrs Lemiers looked hesitantly at Beauchamp, and said, "Do you know anything about clocks?"

"Yes," Beauchamp said. "More than I know about Chinese pottery, in fact."

"There is a grandfather clock in my husband's study. I know nothing about it. Would you mind . . . ?"

"I'd be delighted," Beauchamp grinned.

"It was my father-in-law's," she said, as she led Beauchamp into the study. "I know it's English, but that's all."

Beauchamp took a long appreciative stare at the clock, like a gourmet drinking in the sight of a sumptuous *haute cuisine* dish.

"Gorgeous," he said quietly. "Quite—gorgeous."

"What do you know about it?"

Beauchamp examined the movement, and took a look inside. It was in perfect condition.

"This," he said finally, "is a walnut longcase clock made by a Manchester firm called Thomas Bolton. It was made in 1790, or thereabouts. I would hesitate to value it . . ."

For the first time, Beauchamp saw a flicker of life in Mrs Lemiers' eyes.

"A rough guess," she suggested.

"Four thousand pounds sterling? Probably more. You see, it's a year or two since I dealt in these things, and prices have soared recently. But it's a fabulous piece, and you must have it properly valued at once. The chances are you've under-insured it."

"I think you're right," Mrs Lemiers nodded. "Thank you very much."

"Thank *you*," Beauchamp said. "You've no idea how much pleasure I get from seeing these things."

Mrs Lemiers gazed thoughtfully at her husband's desk.

"I wish I could help you with your search," she said. "You've come all this way."

"It really doesn't matter," Beauchamp said.

"The police took away all my husband's papers. They've sent most of them back, and the rest should be returned next week. Apparently they contain nothing of interest to them, but you're welcome to look at what there is."

She opened the desk drawer and took out several packets of papers which were tied together with string.

"The main order-books are at the company office in Rotterdam. These are various single orders sent in by clients for chemicals."

Beauchamp glanced through them and shook his head.

"Means nothing to me," he admitted. "Did your husband keep a diary, by any chance?"

"Of course," Mrs Lemiers said. "Here."

He looked through the most recent entries, most of which were terse little reminders, such as "Antwerp GTM, 11.30" and "HD Lyons—100 tons H_2SO_4". There were some names and phone numbers, as well, but not those of Carter or anybody else whom Beauchamp was interested in. Nor was there any evidence of a shipment from Naples to England, or anywhere else.

"These notes," Beauchamp said, "I take it they were made during phone calls."

"Yes," Mrs Lemiers nodded. "They're mostly appointments. The rest are orders."

"The orders normally came by phone?"

"Yes, and they'd send written confirmation by post."

"The system worked well, I suppose?"

"Usually," Mrs Lemiers said. "There was a difficult period several months ago with some bad payers. The bank grew nervous, but Pieter managed to sort it out."

"Cash flow," Beauchamp said understandingly. "I know the problem well."

He took another look at the order forms and said, "Presumably, each of the firms in the diary can be identified by looking at the orders. For example, this 'HD Lyons' would be Herschel Daumier S.A. of Lyons, and so on."

"I guess so," Mrs Lemiers said.

Beauchamp put the papers down.

"I wonder if I could ask a favour of you?" he said. "I'm practically convinced that your husband isn't the Lemiers I'm looking for. There seems to be nothing to connect him with my friend. But if I had enough time, I could make quite sure, by looking through this diary and working out where he was on certain dates."

Mrs Lemiers pointed to an armchair.

"Take as long as you want," she said. "You won't be disturbing me."

"That's awfully kind," Beauchamp said. "But it would be a lot easier if I took photocopies of the diary and these orders, and went through them in my own time. I know that business documents are supposed to be confidential, but I promise you I wouldn't—"

"Of course you wouldn't," she interrupted. "Copy as much as you want."

She opened a filing cabinet and took out a small domestic photocopier.

"My gosh," Beauchamp exclaimed. "That's jolly handy."

"My husband was very efficient," she said simply. "Since he died, I've been wondering if he wasn't perhaps a little too efficient for his own good."

"What do you mean?"

She plugged in the photocopier, loaded it with paper, and then looked Beauchamp in the face.

"You say he dealt in arms—"

"I don't know," Beauchamp said hastily. "And I now doubt—"

"It doesn't matter," she said. "Somebody had a reason for killing him. It may have been a burglar, of course. But it wouldn't surprise me if it had something to do with his business."

She took one of the orders and tested the photocopier. It worked.

"I don't think Pieter was a bad man," she said thoughtfully. "But he wasn't totally honest with me. Don't misunderstand, Mr Beauchamp: I'm not angry with him. It's too late for that, anyway, and Pieter gave me little to complain about. We had no children, but there's money and security and . . ."

"I'm terribly sorry," Beauchamp said, and he meant it.

"I'm just trying to say that I don't know everything about Pieter's business life, and it's quite possible that—Anyway, see what you can find."

115

"Thank you," Beauchamp said, and he began to work through the papers. Mrs Lemiers moved towards the door, and then stopped.

"If you like . . ." she said hesitantly.

"Yes?"

"I mean, if you have time, you could stay for dinner. It's—nice to talk."

Beauchamp looked at his watch. The next flight home was in two hours, but there would be others.

"Thank you," he smiled. "I'd like that very much."

TWENTY-SIX

The Laird drank the last of his grappa and asked the waiter for the bill. It had been a pleasant meal, made doubly enjoyable by the article in the *Telegraph*, which the Laird must have re-read at least fifty times.

Of course, the Laird understood that this was a piece of KGB trouble-making: someone in Moscow was merely capitalising on the British government's discomfiture over the Ogden memoirs. The man in the photograph was probably not the real Akhmatov, and the whole thing was almost certainly the work of some cold-blooded bureaucrat in the disinformation department.

But there was a small chance that a retired Soviet spy—a mischievous old codger like Ogden—had understood the point of the hoax and decided to play along, just for the fun of it. The Laird fervently hoped so, and he wished the fellow well.

But not everything was going smoothly, and the Laird was uncomfortably aware of the fact. The meeting with Captain Salvucci that morning had left him feeling baffled and frustrated. What did it all mean? Carter had been diddled—by Lemiers, presumably. But how? How could Lemiers have persuaded Carter that he was a genuine arms dealer? Carter must have found someone who could vouch for the Dutchman—but whom? As Blake had said, nobody in the arms trade had ever heard of Lemiers.

Furthermore, Carter had definitely expected the arms to arrive in Southampton. But according to the captain, Carter had arranged the shipment to Turkey over the phone. This was the most inexplicable part of the whole story. If Carter had sent the ship to Turkey, how could he possibly have been surprised when it failed to appear in Southampton? But if Carter was supposed to be sending arms to an American client, why did he ship them to Turkey? The Laird could only conclude that Carter had somehow swindled himself, but he accepted that this was not a terribly satisfactory explanation.

And what of the Dutchman? It was strange that the captain had never mentioned Lemiers, since according to Blake it was he, and not Carter, who was supposed to have organised the shipment. But according to Captain Salvucci, his only dealings had been with Carter.

Of course, the Laird reflected, the captain had never actually *said* that. He had simply failed to mention Lemiers at all.

"Damn and blast," the Laird muttered. "I suppose I should have raised it with him."

He glanced at his watch. It was eleven-thirty—a little late to disturb the captain, who was probably taking an early night. But this was the Laird's last opportunity to speak to the man. After tonight, Salvucci could be away for weeks—months, possibly. And the captain *had* given the Laird his hotel address . . .

"Sod it," the Laird decided. "I'll pay him a visit. If he gets upset, I'll just buy the man a drink."

He paid his bill and left the restaurant. A passer-by gave him the directions for the Borgo dei Cappuccini, and ten minutes later he was standing in the reception of the Hotel San Marino. There was nobody at the desk, but he could hear sounds coming from a nearby room. He tapped on the door, and found the proprietor and his wife watching a television programme.

"Hello," said the Laird. "Do you speak English, by any chance?"

The man nodded.

"No rooms," he said. "All full."

"Don't want a room," the Laird said. "I'm looking for someone who's staying here. A Captain Salvucci."

"Yes, he is here. But he is asleep. Not to disturb."

"That's all right," the Laird coughed. "He's—em—he's expecting me."

The proprietor grunted sceptically and tapped his wrist-watch.

"Late," he said.

"He won't mind," the Laird persisted. "It's quite important, see? *Molto importante.*"

The proprietor exchanged glances with his wife, and sighed in resignation.

"Okay," he said. "Come with me."

They went up to the third floor, and the proprietor tapped on the captain's door. There was no reply.

"Sleeping," the proprietor observed.

The Laird rapped hard on the door, but there was still no response.

"Maybe he take pill to sleep," the proprietor suggested.

"Wouldn't have thought so," the Laird said. "Those things give you a fuzzy head in the morning, and Salvucci's got a ship to run."

He knocked even harder on the door, but to no avail. The proprietor began to look worried.

"I get key," he muttered. "Wait here."

"All right," the Laird nodded, and he took out his pipe.

A minute later, the proprietor was back with the spare key. He opened the door, and turned on the light. Nothing happened. The proprietor went inside, and cursed as he stumbled into something. Then he found the bedside lamp, and switched it on.

"*Porcodio!*" he exclaimed.

"Christ Almighty," the Laird breathed, and he dropped his pipe on the floor.

The main light had failed to work because the bulb had been removed from it. Its cord now served as a noose, from which the unfortunate Captain Salvucci was swinging over the middle of the room.

TWENTY-SEVEN

"What the fuck is this?" Stringer muttered.

He was reading the transcript of a telephone-tap he had requested some weeks before. It was not a particularly urgent tap, and Stringer had been busy of late, so this was his first opportunity to give the transcript a thorough perusal. He was perplexed by what he read.

The tap had been placed on the phone of a man called Blake, in whom Stringer's department was interested. Sure enough, the opening pages of the transcript consisted of phone calls to and from Mr Blake. But at a certain point, Mr Blake no longer used his own phone, and his voice was replaced by that of someone called Sharon.

Apart from this sudden alteration to the *personae dramatis*, there was a marked change in the subject matter of the phone calls. Mr Blake's conversations had been largely concerned with his illness, and consisted of complaints, hospital appointments, and requests for renewed prescriptions.

But most of Sharon's calls were about a very different subject. It seemed that Sharon was something of a sexual athlete, who distributed her favours among a large crowd of admirers. As one of the phone tappers had noted in an excited marginal comment, "24 of them!!! Where does she get the juice?"

Sharon's stamina was matched by a taste for the esoteric. She and her friends apparently spent a substantial part of their incomes on various Scandinavian appliances whose merits and demerits they discussed in mind-boggling detail. And apart from this mail-order exotica, Sharon had discovered some fascinating new uses for such mundane domestic items as pepper-pots, cheese-graters and marmalade.

After recovering from the initial shock caused by Sharon's lurid conversations, Stringer tried to establish who she was. At first he assumed that she was Blake's daughter, or some other relation, but a quick inspection of Blake's file ruled this out.

120

Blake's daughter was called Annabel, and she lived in Scotland. He had a niece called Janet, who lived abroad. His ex-wife was called Patricia, and she lived in Newcastle. Sharon was not a member of the Blake clan.

It then occurred to Stringer that Sharon was probably a nurse or home-help. But if so, would Blake permit her to make such extraordinary calls, and so many of them, on his phone? It seemed unlikely. Besides, there was no indication in Blake's original calls that anyone called Sharon was about to move into his home.

The one remaining possibility was that Blake had gone away, and that Sharon was some sort of holiday tenant or house-minder. This would certainly explain why Sharon never referred to Blake in her calls, or even alluded to him. But this too seemed improbable. Once again, Blake's calls gave no indication that he was about to leave home, and there was no mention of any future tenant.

In short, Sharon was a complete mystery. Stringer phoned the tapping centre, and asked to speak to Kevin, who was responsible for this particular piece of surveillance.

"Hello?" Kevin said.

"This is Stringer, in Curzon Street. Are you the man in charge of the Blake tap?"

"That's me."

"What the hell's going on?" Stringer demanded. "I asked for a transcript, not a pornographic novel."

Stringer could make out a muffled snigger at the other end of the line.

"Not my fault, guv," Kevin said. "What you've got is what we heard."

"I know *that*," Stringer said. "I'm not accusing you of making it up—"

"I couldn't, guv," Kevin giggled. 'I doubt if anyone could."

"I'm just saying there's been some kind of mistake."

"What do you mean?"

Stringer took a deep breath.

"Look," he said patiently, "we asked for a tap on a guy called Blake, right?"

"Right."

"And we got one—until page twelve. Then Blake disappears, and we get some nymphomaniac called Sharon instead."

"What about it?"

"Well, didn't it occur to you that Sharon's on another line? That you've been tapping the wrong phone?"

There was a pause, and Kevin said, "No, guv. To tell the truth, it didn't."

Stringer's eyeballs rolled upwards in exasperation.

"It does occur to me, Kevin," he said heavily. "And it occurs to me that there's been a cock-up."

"You think so?" Kevin said. "I can't see how, myself. We got the right phone, didn't we? That's Blake at the beginning of the sheet. Now nobody's moved the tap—"

"Are you sure about that?"

"Of course I'm sure," Kevin snorted. "That exchange is in the middle of nowhere, guv. Since we fitted the tap, none of our people's been round there. We've never done a job there before, and we'll probably never do one again."

"Perhaps it was one of the exchange staff," Stringer suggested, "tinkering round with the wires."

"Seems unlikely," Kevin said. "The line was given the standard red fuse, meaning 'do not touch'. And if they did tamper with it, they'd have disconnected it, not transferred it somewhere else."

"You're sure about that?"

"Course I am. And I can tell you, guv, nothing like that's ever happened before."

Stringer paused for thought. Kevin was clearly an oaf, but he presumably knew his business. And Stringer, too, had never heard of such a case before. But the tap had better be checked, just in case.

"I'm sorry, Kevin, but you'll just have to go back and look in the exchange—"

"Oh, leave it out, guv," Kevin groaned.

"Kevin . . ."

"Have you any idea how busy we are? We're overloaded with orders, guv, and we can't handle what we've got. I can't afford to send a man on a trip down to Kent just for one inspection."

"Please, Kevin."

"I tell you what," Kevin said, "day after tomorrow, we've got a bloke going to Folkestone. If you can hang on 'til then . . ."

"All right," Stringer conceded. "But I want to hear immediately, understand? The minute he knows."

"Yeah, guv. Will do."

"Thanks," Stringer said.

"But I can tell you now," Kevin added, "there's nothing wrong."

"Let's see, shall we?"

"Yeah. But I bet there's a really simple answer to all this. One you've never thought of."

"Really," Stringer said drily. "Any suggestions?"

"As a matter of fact, I have," Kevin said. "Me and the lads have been giving it some thought, and . . ."

"Go on."

"Well, we think Blake's had a sex-change operation."

"*What?*"

"A sex-change," Kevin repeated, "and he's now called Sharon—"

"Oh, for Christ's sake . . ."

"Why not?" Kevin demanded. "I mean, that explains why he made all those calls to the hospital—"

"Thanks, Kevin."

"All those prescriptions must be for hormone tablets—"

"Goodbye, Kevin."

Stringer put the phone down, and shook his head wearily.

"Pillock," he said.

TWENTY-EIGHT

The Laird was not enjoying life. After finding Captain Salvucci's body, he had spent most of the night at the Livorno police station. The young detective in charge of the murder inquiry had no other suspects to interview, and he subjected the Laird to many hours of intensive questioning.

With some difficulty, the Laird tried to explain the nature of his visit to the captain's room, and why he had come to Livorno in the first place. He told the detective that he had come in search of a missing arms shipment for Southampton which in fact had not gone missing at all, but was really a cargo of fertiliser which had gone to Turkey instead. Or so the Laird thought, but he couldn't be entirely sure because he was not convinced that the chap who arranged the shipment really knew what he had arranged, and it was quite possible that this fellow was the victim of some skulduggery by another chap who *should* have arranged the shipment, but apparently hadn't.

Not surprisingly, the detective was somewhat puzzled by all this, and matters were not helped by his shaky grasp of English. Of course, he realised it was improbable that this cantankerous old Englishman could have overpowered and throttled a strong man half his age. The Laird was built along generous lines, but most of his youthful muscle had long ago turned to lard.

But the Laird did his own case little good by calling the detective a pea-brained cloth-eared spaghetti-eating wop fool. The detective was understandably miffed by this, and since he had nothing else to go on, he detained the Laird for over seven hours, until the pathologist announced Captain Salvucci's time of death. The restaurant had confirmed that the Laird was half-way through his *antipasto* at the time in question, so the detective had no choice but to release his guest with a vague caution about keeping out of trouble in future.

The Laird shuffled wearily back to his hotel, and wondered if Sybil's constant strictures were not entirely groundless: he really

124

was too old for this sort of thing, and even Clive Ogden's sense of fun would have deserted him after a night in an Italian police station.

But after a few hours' sleep and several cups of *espresso*, the Laird began to recover his enthusiasm. After all, things had taken an intriguing new twist. People were being bumped off, presumably to ensure their silence. But silence about what? The captain had been entirely frank, but had revealed nothing remotely dangerous or incriminating. A routine delivery of agricultural goods to the other end of the Mediterranean—what was so sinister about that? And if the captain's story was true, why should anyone wish to remove him?

In that case, the Laird concluded, the captain must have been lying. Some part of his story had been invented—but which? The Laird was no authority on shipping matters, and he had no idea how to confirm or disprove what he had been told. But then . . .

There was *one* thing, the Laird recalled, which could be checked fairly easily. Captain Salvucci had claimed that his cargo had been checked by the port authorities at Naples—a routine inspection, the captain had said. If so, there must be some record of the inspection, and the Laird could make certain that it really had occurred. Because if it hadn't, it would follow that the captain had lied, and that the cargo might well have contained guns after all.

"To Naples," the Laird decided, and he went off to pack his luggage.

The train journey took several hours, and was delayed by one of the regular Italian railway strikes. By the time the Laird arrived in Naples it was dark, and he had no choice but to put off his inquiry until the following morning. So he spent the rest of the day in restaurants and bars, and by the time he went to bed life did not seem quite so arduous, after all.

The next day, the port authorities did not exactly fall over each other in the rush to assist with the Laird's inquiries. The Laird was irritated by their lack of enthusiasm, and when they reminded him that Naples was one of the world's great sea-ports and suggested that the activities of one small freighter were of trifling concern to them, he threw a minor tantrum in their office.

Unfortunately, tantrums are an everyday feature of Neapolitan

125

life, and the officials were not persuaded to change their minds. But one charitable secretary, who spoke excellent English, took pity on the excitable old man, and sat him down with a cup of coffee and an offer to do what she could.

She went away and returned twenty minutes later with a collection of photocopied documents. These were the records of the inspection carried out by the harbour police on the SS *Flavio* shortly before it left on its last journey to Greece, Turkey and Cyprus.

"About bloody time," the Laird said, by way of thanks. "What does it say?"

"The cargo was in order. Everything was as described on the ship's manifest."

The Laird groaned in disappointment.

"You sure about that?"

"Of course."

"There were no guns, or explosives, or anything like that?"

The secretary gazed at the Laird incredulously.

"Guns?" she repeated.

"Yes, guns. Bang-bang. Boom-boom. You know."

She smiled and held out the document.

"See for yourself. You may keep these, if you wish."

"Thanks," grunted the Laird, and he read through the list. It was little more than a list of chemicals.

"Potassium hydrogen fluoride, two tons; phosphorus oxychloride, six tons; hydrogen fluoride, five tons . . . no guns."

"No guns," she smiled.

"But—but did they check the chemical drums? Did they actually look inside?"

"These are thorough inspections. Several containers would have been picked at random and checked."

"I see. Well, thanks anyway."

"My pleasure," the secretary smiled.

The Laird returned to his hotel, with a heavy heart. It really did appear that the captain was telling the truth. There were no guns—at least, there were none on the SS *Flavio*. And it was most probable that the captain had not been lying about anything else, which made his murder seem doubly inexplicable.

The Laird realised that there was nothing further he could do in Italy, and that it was time to go home. Perhaps it was the latest disappointment, perhaps it was the shock of the captain's murder, but for some reason he had lost all inclination to do any sightseeing. Italy was a jolly nice place, of course, but he would enjoy it better on a more conventional holiday. With a depressing sense of failure, and a touch of indigestion brought on by all the good food, the Laird made his way to the airport.

TWENTY-NINE

Stringer was in a bad mood. Much of Stringer's life was spent in this condition, though there were occasional cheerful interludes. These were becoming increasingly rare, and the bad mood was beginning to show signs of permanence. Firstly, there was all that hassle with the memoirs of that old bastard Ogden. Then there were those bastard Russians, who had decided to play along with the old bastard Ogden and produce another old bastard to verify the old bastard's stories. And now . . .

"How did it happen?" he demanded. "How could it happen?"

"No idea, guv," Kevin said, waving his hands helplessly. "Honestly, me and the lads are well gutted by this one—"

"Tell me about it," Stringer scoffed, as he lit a cigarette.

"Fair dos, guv," Kevin pleaded. "How could we know some bugger had switched the tap? Never happened before."

Stringer blew a large cloud of smoke into Kevin's face.

"So you said," he nodded. "I want to know how, Kevin."

"Must have been an accident. Some geezer at the exchange undone the connections on the frame and . . . and . . ."

"You told me that couldn't happen," Stringer reminded him. "You said the most likely thing would be that the tap was disconnected altogether."

"Yeah," Kevin said lamely. "I did say that, didn't I?"

"Yes you fucking well did," Stringer shouted. "But it wasn't disconnected, was it? It was fucking well moved. And the chances are it was fucking well done on purpose."

Kevin blinked in surprise. This possibility had not occurred to him.

"Are you saying some geezer at the exchange *knew* it was a tap and . . ."

Stringer clapped his hands in sarcastic praise.

"Full marks, Kevin."

"Well, fuck me sideways," Kevin said, scratching his scalp. "Why'd anyone do a thing like that?"

"I don't know," Stringer admitted. "But you're going to find out."

Kevin grinned weakly.

"It *must* have been an accident, guv. Honestly, I don't think that—"

"I don't give a shit what you think," Stringer interrupted. "Your half-arsed opinions just don't interest me, Kevin. I asked for a tap on Blake, and what did I get?"

He picked up the tap transcript and waved it truculently under Kevin's nose.

"This crap," he spat. "Pages and pages of bullshit about some housewife with the itch. Someone's been taking the piss out of me, Kevin, and it makes me bloody angry."

"Does it?" Kevin gasped. "I mean—yeah, I suppose it would."

"I want to know who's been taking the piss, Kevin. I want to know fast. Get me?"

"Fair enough," Kevin nodded. "But . . ."

"But what?"

"Could take a while to find out. I mean, we've got to talk to the day *and* night staff at the exchange—"

"Do it."

"Yeah, but that might mean the police get to hear—"

"Do it," Stringer repeated. "Interference with phone lines is a criminal offence."

"True, but we don't want the publicity, guv. You know how we work: it's all on the q.t. If this gets public—"

"That's your problem," Stringer said simply.

Kevin sagged in despair.

"Oh, leave it out, guv. If the newspapers hear about this, we'll all be in the brown and sticky, know what I mean?"

"Speak for yourself," Stringer said nastily.

"You too, guv," Kevin insisted. "Because if my boss asks me why there's a newspaper article about government phone-taps being switched around, I'm going to tell him—"

"Tell him whatever you like," Stringer offered. "His bollocks are on the line as well. You said it yourself, Kevin: these things just don't happen. And if I make a big smell about this in *my* boss's office, a lot of people are going to wind up singing falsetto in the church choir. Get it?"

At once, Kevin's face turned several shades paler.

"You couldn't," he choked. "I mean, that would be fucking *dire*."

The thought of a formal complaint to the Director-General of MI5 about a major surveillance fiasco made Kevin feel decidedly ill.

"Do me a favour, guv," Kevin said imploringly. "Have you any idea what kind of aggravation we'd suffer if—"

"I couldn't give a monkey's," Stringer said. "Just find out who did it."

Kevin took a deep breath. All his instincts told him that such disasters were best put down to experience, and then quietly forgotten. An investigation of the kind Stringer was proposing would only lead to trouble, and Kevin wanted a quiet life.

"All right, guv," he said. "But think about this: if you're right, and the tap *was* switched on purpose—"

"Which it was."

"Then whoever done it probably had something to do with the target of the tap—wassisname, Blake—right?"

Stringer said nothing.

"And if that's true," Kevin reasoned, "then you're more likely to suss out who done it than we are. I mean, you know all about this geezer Blake, don't you? You've got all the gen on him."

Stringer nodded thoughtfully. Kevin had a point: the job had almost certainly been carried out by a professional, but it may have been someone in Mr Blake's employ. In which case, it was to Mr Blake's file that an investigator should go.

"Fair enough, Kevin," Stringer said quietly. "But even if the switch was done by somebody from outside the exchange—"

"Must have been," Kevin said.

"—they must still have been let into the exchange by one of the staff."

"I suppose so," Kevin said reluctantly.

"So you can find out who let them in and why. Once you've done that, leave it with me."

"All right. But it could take a week or two—"

"It won't," Stringer said firmly. "You've got one week."

"One week!" Kevin howled. "Jesus Christ, guv, that's well out of order. Be reasonable . . ."

"I'm being fucking reasonable," Stringer snarled. "And if you don't think so, just wait and see what happens when I'm unreasonable. I can be a real bastard, Kevin."

Kevin was not inclined to argue this point.

"Okay, guv," he sighed. "One week. But I'm not promising nothing."

Stringer put out his cigarette.

"Yes you are, Kevin," he said calmly. "You're promising me that you'll find the person who let our guy into the exchange. And if I don't hear that person's name inside one week—well, just think about that church choir, eh?"

THIRTY

"Try these pork thingies," Ogden suggested. "They're in a very good whatsit sauce—"

"A black bean sauce," Sybil said.

"That's the one," Ogden agreed. "Jolly tasty."

Ogden & Co. were having dinner in a Chinese restaurant, to celebrate everybody's safe return from their trips abroad. As Ogden said, the food was "jolly tasty", and they were all piling in vigorously, save for the Vicar, who had not yet mastered the use of chopsticks.

"Can't get the hang of them," he said, as they dropped into the sweet-and-sour for the umpteenth time.

"It's perfectly simple, Godfrey," Sybil said. "Even you can do it. Watch me."

The Vicar studied his wife as her chopsticks darted backwards and forwards among the bowls of food.

"It's no good," he sighed. "I'll have to get a knife and fork. Waiter . . . ?"

"Did you enjoy America, Clive?" the Laird asked.

"Terrific," Ogden said. "Loved every bit of it. You know, American bubble-gum is far better than anything you can buy here: amazing multi-coloured goo that forms the most extraordinary patterns when you blow. I bought another suitcase so I could bring home half a ton of the stuff."

"What about the sights?" Beauchamp inquired. "Or were you too busy in the sweet-shops to notice?"

"On the contrary, I did a great deal of sightseeing. Disneyland was fabulous, though I'm told that Disney World is even better. But that's in Florida, which wasn't on my route, so next time I'm going to make a point of—"

"Are you saying you spent all your trip visiting children's amusement parks?" Sybil asked incredulously.

"Unfortunately, no," Ogden admitted. "I had to waste a great deal of time speaking to newspapers and television people.

Shame, really; if it hadn't been for those characters, I might have had time to nip down to Florida. Still, all play and no work makes Jack a credit risk, what?"

"D'you hear about Akhmatov?" the Laird said.

"Of course," Ogden grinned. "Wasn't that hilarious? Some American TV company showed me a video recording of the interview. I'm fairly sure that was the real Akhmatov, you know. That emaciated, pasty face looked just like the chap I remembered. I wonder what our old friend Stringer thought when he heard about it."

"I bet he blew a gasket," the Vicar said. "There were questions in Parliament about it, and it was pretty obvious that someone was due for a carpeting."

"Well, let's hope it's Stringer," Beauchamp said. "Couldn't happen to a nicer fellow."

"Hear, hear," cried the Laird.

"Death to all footballers," the Vicar murmured.

"Anyway," Ogden said, "let's recap on everything we've learned, and see what we can make of it. Firstly, I've discovered that Magnum Inc. is a CIA front which is no longer running, and whose owner has buggered off.

"Secondly, the Laird has discovered that the SS *Flavio* never ran arms, but shipped agricultural chemicals instead. We know this because the boat was inspected in Naples. Furthermore, the boat was never destined for Southampton, but went instead to Greece and Turkey. The job was apparently ordered by Carter, and not Lemiers as was originally thought. Furthermore, the captain has been murdered for no clear reason.

"Thirdly, Jeremy has found *a* Pieter Lemiers, but not necessarily *the* Lemiers. Jeremy's Lemiers dealt in chemicals, travelled a lot, and was also murdered for no apparent reason. Right, chaps, what do we make of all this?"

"The first question," Beauchamp said, "is whether or not my Lemiers is our man. At first, it seemed that he was. We had one point of connection—the *Flavio*'s cargo was ordered by a Lemiers who would send it in chemical drums. My Lemiers could certainly have done that. But unfortunately, the Laird's blown a hole in that."

"Lemiers didn't order the cargo," the Laird nodded. "Carter did."

133

"Exactly," Ogden said. "And even if Lemiers did put chemicals on the *Flavio*, that's no bloody help to us. After all, the goods were supposed to be arms, not chemicals. Carter dealt in arms, and so did the Americans. They wanted guns and bombs, not fly-spray and artificial manure."

"And they wanted it in Southampton, not Turkey," the Vicar observed. "But the captain said Carter sent the boat to Mersin. What do you make of that?"

"Nothing, at present," Ogden admitted. "Let's stick to Lemiers, for the time being. It seems he didn't order the boat—is there anything which might tie him in with this, Jeremy?"

"Not really. According to his diary, my Lemiers was in Paris for at least two of the days when Carter was dealing with his Lemiers. But on other days, he was in Holland, Belgium and Switzerland. There's nothing conclusive. And there's no mention of Carter's name or phone number in there."

"What about the other stuff in the diary?"

"I've identified almost all of it. They're all European chemical manufacturers who did regular business with my Lemiers' firm. The only one I couldn't identify was the name SEPP. The word appears several times on its own. In one place it also says PO Box 5367, but there's no town or country. Elsewhere the words '2 more tons POC13' are written beside it. I suppose SEPP is just another client—perhaps someone working for one of Lemiers' client companies."

"Did any of the names in the diary match those on the *Flavio*'s documents?" the Laird asked. "Those delivery notes Captain Salvucci showed me and the Turkish agent's receipt."

"No," Beauchamp said. "There were two destinations at the Mersin end: Egridir Fertilisers in Turkey, and the State Organisation for Chemical Industries in Iraq. Neither of them appears in any of Lemiers' papers."

"So when you examine the matter closely," Ogden concluded, "there's really nothing to connect Jeremy's Lemiers with our inquiry."

"I knew it," Sybil said triumphantly. "You pestered that poor widow for nothing."

"I didn't pester her," Beauchamp said indignantly. "As a matter of fact, we got on very well."

"What did you chat about?" the Vicar grinned. "Antiques?"

"If you must know, yes."

"Oh dear," Ogden said, with a pained smile. "Anyway, where were we? If we delete Jeremy's Lemiers from our list, what does that leave us with? A cargo of guns that were really chemicals, sent to Turkey when they should have gone to Southampton and America. Rather baffling, eh?"

"Time for a theory," the Vicar suggested.

"Fire away, Vicar."

"We started off on the assumption that Carter was the victim of a hoax. Let's stick to that. The aim of the hoax was to swindle an arms dealer out of a large sum of money, and it worked. Lemiers—whoever he was—told Carter he could supply arms. Carter believed him."

"But why?" the Laird asked. "Lemiers had no references, no contacts—"

"It doesn't matter," the Vicar said. "He may have used forged documents or something, but the fact is he did it."

"Quite right," Ogden said. "Keep going, Vicar."

"You'll remember," the Vicar said, "that this was supposed to be an illegal delivery, with no end-user certificate. So Lemiers said he would put the arms on a certain ship, disguised as chemicals. Lemiers then found the name of a ship which regularly ran shipments of chemicals, and told Carter that this boat would be doing the job.

"Furthermore, to make the story watertight, Lemiers told Carter he could even watch the chemicals being loaded onto the ship. So Carter did exactly that, not realising that the drums he saw loaded really did contain chemicals.

"But of course the ship never came to Southampton, and by the time Carter found out, it was too late. Lemiers had vanished with Carter's money, and was now untraceable."

"Not bad," Ogden said. "But I can see some major flaws. Firstly, Lemiers didn't originally know it was going to be an illegal job. That only came about when Colonel Kyle placed his order. If Carter had found a legitimate customer for the arms, he would have expected the guns to be shipped normally, and he could have inspected them for himself."

"True," the Vicar conceded. "But then Lemiers would have found another way of diddling him."

The others were not convinced.

"You're also ignoring one thing," the Laird said. "Captain Salvucci claimed that Carter had ordered the shipment, not Lemiers."

"I've thought about that," the Vicar said. "The captain said that before he met Carter on that one occasion at Naples, he'd only dealt with him by phone."

"So what?"

"Perhaps it wasn't Carter who'd spoken to him. Perhaps it was someone claiming to be Carter."

"Surely he could tell their voices apart?"

"Not necessarily. International phone lines can be quite bad, and the Laird says that the captain's English wasn't the best."

"That's an interesting point," Ogden said.

"That's utter rubbish," Sybil said. "Pure speculation."

"Not really," the Vicar said. "How else do you account for the fact that Carter sent the ship to Turkey and then waited for it in Southampton?"

"But haven't you contradicted yourself?" Beauchamp said. "Firstly you suggested that Lemiers merely found out about somebody else's chemical shipment. Now you're saying he arranged it. Which is it to be?"

"The first," the Vicar said. "But there's no contradiction: Lemiers found out about a shipment from company X to the SS *Flavio*, all right? Then he phoned the *Flavio*'s captain and claimed to be a director of company X. He asked a few routine questions, like 'what time will you be loading the stuff on board?', and said he'd be there to see it off. Provided there were no hitches with the delivery, there was no reason for Captain Salvucci to phone company X and ask to speak to a Mr Carter."

"Fair enough," the Laird said, "but wasn't Lemiers taking a big risk? He invited Carter to watch the stuff being loaded: what if Carter chatted to the captain about their phone call? What if he said 'see you in Southampton'?"

The Vicar smiled gleefully.

"But he didn't, did he? Carter just said 'see you at the other end'. Then he sat on the dock, and didn't say another word, and Lemiers jolly well knew he wouldn't. Remember, this was an illegal shipment, and Carter wasn't going to take any risks. He was far too nervous."

The others fell silent, and weighed up the pros and cons of the Vicar's theory. It wasn't perfect, but it was the best thing on offer.

"This is all very well," Ogden said, "but it fails to explain one important thing. Why have several people connected with this swindle been murdered? There's Carter, the investigator, and now Captain Salvucci."

"Not to mention Jeremy's Lemiers," the Laird said.

"He doesn't count," Ogden said. "We've ruled him out, and his death isn't a coincidence. Remember, Jeremy heard about him from a policeman, precisely because he'd been murdered. But there's nothing about his murder to link him with the others."

"Quite the reverse," Beauchamp said. "Lemiers was the only one who was shot. The others were all killed by other means."

"Exactly," Ogden said. "But how does the Vicar's theory explain the other three?"

"Carter was swindled," the Vicar said, "but the only loser was his client, Colonel Kyle."

"Are you saying Kyle's taking revenge?"

"Why not?"

"Seems most improbable," Ogden said. "After all, by ordinary standards, Magnum Inc. lost a lot of money. But by CIA standards, it was nothing. Petty cash. And if this is all revenge, it's pretty cack-handed. Carter wasn't guilty of any-thing—"

"The Americans might not have seen it that way," the Vicar said.

"But why murder the private investigator, Hopkins, or Captain Salvucci? What had they done to upset the Americans?"

"Nothing," the Vicar conceded. "All right, so it wasn't revenge. But whatever the real reason is, I bet it fits in with my theory."

Sybil's patience finally ran out.

"Godfrey," she said, "your so-called theory is the most ridicu-lous piece of tripe I have ever heard."

"Yes, dear," the Vicar sighed.

"It's utter piffle, and you know it."

"If you say so, dear."

"Now finish your meal before it gets cold."

"Yes, dear."

"Murders by the CIA, indeed!" Sybil scoffed. "Why, you'll next be telling me that this colonel's going to come here and murder us all in our beds. Really!"

THIRTY-ONE

Colonel Brutus Kyle looked around the reception of his hotel. It was one of the more opulent establishments in Mayfair, but that did not mean anything to him. To judge from the expression on the colonel's face, London was not to his taste.

"Why hast thou made us come up out of Egypt, to bring us to this evil place?" he muttered. "It is no place for grain, or figs, or vines, or pomegranates."

"If you'd just sign here," the receptionist said, pointing to a line in the guest book.

Colonel Kyle took a pen and wrote something down. The receptionist glanced at the entry, and said, "Thank you very much Mr . . . er, Mr Word. Is that your name: Mr Word?"

"Then I saw heaven opened," the colonel quoted, "and behold, a white horse! He who sat upon it is called Faithful and True, and the name by which he is called is the Word of God."

"I see," the receptionist said calmly. "Well, thank you, Mr Word. I hope you enjoy your stay in London. Philip here will show you to your room."

The bell-boy took Colonel Kyle's bag and escorted him to the lift.

"Are you here on business or pleasure, sir?" he inquired, as they got out on the fourth floor. "You don't look like a tourist, if I may say so."

"Tourist?" the colonel repeated. "Ha! Vanity of vanities, says the Preacher, vanity of vanities! All is vanity and a striving after wind."

The bell-boy nodded laconically.

"Didn't think you were a tourist. Here's your room."

He opened the door and they went inside. Colonel Kyle did not bother to look around to see if things were to his liking. He went to the window and gazed down at the traffic.

"Everything okay then, sir?" the bell-boy inquired.

The colonel did not reply.

"If there's anything you want . . ."

Like most of his type, the bell-boy expected to be tipped. Indeed, he prided himself on never leaving a guest's room without first receiving some gratuity, however small.

"First time in London, sir?" he asked. "If you've any time to spare, I can tell you of a few places to spend it. Clubs, bars. Something a bit daring, perhaps? The sort of places you business-men like to unwind in . . ."

The colonel continued to gaze through the window.

"You didn't say what your business here was, sir," the bell-boy observed. "Perhaps I could . . ."

Colonel Kyle turned round and stared down at the boy.

"My business?" he repeated.

"Yes. Why you've come to London."

"As the psalm says, 'insolent men have risen against me,'" the colonel explained. "'A band of ruthless men seek my life.'"

"Crikey! Have you told the police?"

The colonel laughed disdainfully, as if the police were the last people who could help him.

"So what are you going to do?" the bell-boy said.

"Harass the Midianites and smite them," the colonel said, "for they have harassed me with their wiles."

"You don't say? Do you know where they are?"

The colonel shook his head ruefully.

"But every one who asks, receives," he said. "And he who seeks, finds."

"I like your confidence," the bell-boy grinned. "Now, if that'll be all . . ."

He held out his hand. Colonel Kyle misunderstood the gesture: he took the boy's hand and shook it firmly.

"Take heed and beware of the leaven of the Pharisees and the Sadducees," was the colonel's parting advice.

"Right!" the bell-boy gasped. "I'll—I'll bear that in mind, sir."

He abandoned any hope of a tip, and hurriedly left the room.

THIRTY-TWO

Sybil rolled over and turned on her bedside lamp. With a disconsolate snort, she put on her glasses and blinked sleepily at the alarm clock. It was four in the morning. In the last five hours she had accrued a total of fifty minutes' sleep.

It must have been something she had eaten at the Chinese restaurant. Every few seconds her abdomen emitted a low, cavernous rumble, accompanied by random creaks and a chorus of high-pitched squeals.

After five hours of this visceral cacophony, Sybil gave up. There was no point in trying to sleep through such a ferocious intestinal blitzkrieg, particularly when it was accompanied by the sound-effects from her husband's bedroom. It was over twenty years since the Vicar's fine baritone snore had caused him to be banished from the matrimonial suite, but the sound was still powerful enough to penetrate the walls of Sybil's boudoir. Tonight she found it doubly exasperating, since it showed that the Chinese meal was having no ill-effects on her spouse. It was jolly unfair, Sybil decided.

She got out of bed, put on her gown, and went downstairs to the kitchen. There she took out several rusty old tins containing the remnants of various brands of stomach-powder, all of which had long ago been taken off the market. Sybil swore by these brands, and was convinced that the only reason they were no longer on sale was because they tasted unpleasant, and people expected to be mollycoddled nowadays. Sybil belonged to a generation with strong views on the subject of medicine: all good remedies were either horribly painful, foul-smelling, or left a vile taste in the mouth. The best ones left the patient half-dead.

She poured the powders into a glass, and watched in satisfaction as the water turned a menacing, stagnant-pond khaki. She drank it in one gulp, and at once she felt gratifyingly bilious. After five minutes the nausea subsided, and the Chinese meal was *hors de combat*.

Unfortunately, Sybil no longer felt particularly sleepy. She decided to move to the drawing-room and read a book for a little while. She was half-way through a large tome by an obscure Edwardian novelist: the story was absurd and the characters were incredible, but the world described was a better one than Sybil inhabited, and it reminded her of a time—not so very long ago—when people were sensible, and did precisely what was expected of them.

But as she opened the book, she could not help noticing the documents left behind by the Vicar's friends. The papers lay in an untidy heap on the coffee-table: photocopies, handwritten notes, and strange diagrams.

They really are an overgrown bunch of boy scouts, Sybil thought. It was quite improper for a group of retired gentlemen to go snooping around like a firm of seedy private investigators. Respectable people minded their own business. It was all that man Ogden's fault, and Sybil wished fervently that her husband's friend would be struck down by a minor heart attack, or a chronic bout of arthritis, or something equally crippling. Nothing lethal, of course—Sybil was not malicious—but debilitating enough to put a stop to his puerile activities. The man was far too healthy for his own good.

It wasn't as if the men were particularly competent at what they were doing. Sybil knew that she could make a far better job of investigating the missing armaments and the subsequent murders—assuming that she wanted to, of course, and Sybil had no such inclination. But it was clear that the men did not know how to interpret the information they had amassed. The work needed a clear head and lots of common sense. The men lacked both these qualities, but Sybil had them in abundance.

Without doubt, Ogden & Co. had overlooked some important clues. Sybil could not remember what, exactly, but she knew they had ignored a point of interest. It was something Jeremy Beauchamp had said—but what, exactly?

Sybil shook her head. She had no choice but to look at the papers. After a few moments of rummaging, she found the reminder. It was a note in the Laird's handwriting which contained the destination of the *Flavio*'s chemical shipment. Some of it was going to Egridir Fertilisers in Turkey, and the rest was going to the State Organisation for Chemical Industries

142

in Baghdad. The men had taken this information for granted, but Sybil remembered that it had struck a chord in her. But why? It really was too late at night . . .

That was it! The Turkish shipment meant nothing to her, but the other destination—Baghdad—was quite interesting. It reminded her of a newspaper article she had read. Or was it a television programme? Anyway, it was worth looking into. It could be another red herring, of course, but she could check it easily and at no expense. And that was more than could be said for the extravagant jaunts Ogden & Co. had taken recently.

Of course, all this assumed that Sybil was prepared to do the men's work for them. Her first instinct was to forget all about the matter.

But, she reflected, there were other considerations. The sooner this business was resolved, the sooner she and her husband could return to the business of being a normal, retired couple. If Ogden & Co. were left to their own devices, the saga might drag on for ever. At the end of their meal, the men had decided to present their findings to Mr Blake. If he was unsatisfied with the Vicar's theory, they would press on with the inquiry. And there was no doubt that Mr Blake would be unsatisfied: the man wanted to know why his partner had been killed, and the Vicar's theory had yet to account for *that* little enigma. So the whole sorry affair would plague Sybil for months to come—years, perhaps—unless she stepped in and sorted it out with the aid of her powerful, no-nonsense intellect.

Besides, Sybil would derive grim satisfaction from out-sleuthing these amateur sleuths. It would prove once and for all that she was a person to be taken seriously. Oh yes, Sybil knew what the men said behind her back. It was quite clear from the impertinent twinkle in Clive Ogden's eyes that she was a figure of fun to him. Well, she would jolly well show *him*.

She looked up at the clock over the mantelpiece. It was now a quarter to five. She no longer felt sleepy—indeed, her latest decision seemed to have instilled new energy into her. She picked up the papers from the coffee-table once more, put a pad of paper on her lap, and began to take tidy, methodical notes.

THIRTY-THREE

A room in the police station had been set aside for Stringer's use. The police in this part of Kent were not accustomed to receiving visits from "London high-ups", and they felt highly flattered by Stringer's presence. Stringer regarded them as a bunch of country bumpkins, and he treated them as such, but this only prompted further displays of grovelling servility from his hosts.

"We've got Jack Goodhart here, sir," the duty sergeant said. "Now if there's anything you want—coffee, tea—just call me. The Inspector's got a bottle of something stronger, if you feel like that, and—"

"Just show the guy in," Stringer said flatly.

"Right you are, sir."

The sergeant scuttled off, leaving Stringer to reflect wearily on the leisurely pace of rural life.

"Bloody hayseed," he muttered.

After several days of careful investigation, Kevin's inquiries had borne fruit: one of the night staff at the phone exchange had recently admitted two "special engineers" for whom no records could be found. Almost certainly, these were the people who had interfered with the tap on Mr Blake's line. Now Stringer was about to interview the man who had let them in, in the hope of gleaning further clues about their identity.

"Jack Goodhart, sir," the sergeant said, as he showed in the bewildered phone engineer. "If there's anything else you need—"

"I'll call you," Stringer said. "Thanks."

"Use that phone," the sergeant said, pointing to one of two phones on the desk. "The other one's out of order—"

"Sergeant," Stringer said heavily, "do me a favour and piss off, will you?"

"Yes sir," the sergeant said humbly, and he withdrew from the office.

"Right," Stringer said briskly. "Your name's Jack Goodhart, yes?"

The other man nodded.

"I don't know what this is about, squire . . ."

"You were doing the night shift at your exchange on the night of Friday the twenty—"

"Is this about them two special engineers?"

"Just answer the questions, Jack," Stringer advised. "We'll get through it quicker that way."

"I'm entitled to a lawyer," Jack said. "I know my rights. The police have to offer you a solicitor before—"

"Bollocks," Stringer said elegantly. "For starters, I'm not a cop."

"You're not?"

"No. And nobody's charging you with anything. I just want some information, see?"

"Yeah," Jack said, but he sounded far from convinced.

"But I'll tell you this," Stringer added. "Ever since I came here, I've been pissed around by just about everybody I've met, and I'm getting a bit bored with it."

"Sorry to hear it," Jack murmured.

"So am I Jack, so am I. And if you piss me around as well, I'm going to lose my patience. Like I say, Jack, I'm not a cop, and I can't arrest you. But if you don't tell me everything you know at the first time of asking, I can get somebody else to arrest you on any one of a dozen charges."

"Such as?"

"Accessory to any one of twenty crimes, conspiracy to interfere with the telephone system—"

"Conspiracy?" Jack howled. "Come off it, squire."

"Well, if you don't help me," Stringer reasoned, "it must be because you're helping the villains."

"I'm not," Jack insisted.

"In that case, tell me what you know about them. What did they look like?"

"There was two of them," Jack said. "They were both old geezers—"

"How old?"

"Sixty-five, seventy? Something like that."

"*What?*" Stringer exclaimed.

"You heard me."

Stringer scratched his head.

"Jack," he asked, "what's the retirement age in your line of work?"

"Sixty, usually."

"Didn't you think these guys might be a little old for that sort of job?"

"Sure," Jack said. "But their ID was in order. They were driving the right kind of van—one of the Reserve-fleet jobs. And them special engineers aren't like the rest of us, anyway. I don't know when they retire."

Stringer sighed, and began to take notes.

"You say their ID was all right. Did you check it?"

"Not closely," Jack admitted.

"Did you *read* it?"

"No," Jack said hesitantly. "Not really."

Stringer looked upwards in disgust.

"Not really," he repeated. "Christ Almighty."

"Well, like I say, their van was for real, and—"

"Sure," Stringer said understandingly. "I don't know why we bother with ID cards. We should just give everybody a van instead. Problem solved, eh Jack?"

Jack shifted uncomfortably.

"Did they tell you what they were doing?" Stringer asked.

"No," Jack said. "Just like the last lot. They asked me to make them coffee, and that was it."

"You say they were old men. Can you give me a more detailed description?"

Jack screwed up his eyes in concentration.

"Well," he said, "they were both posh. Well spoken, you know?"

Stringer nodded.

"Carry on."

"One of them was about my height. Had a gammy leg, I think."

"He walked with a limp?"

"Yeah, just slightly. And the other one was taller. A lot taller, as a matter of fact. Well over six foot. Quite skinny."

Stringer wrote this down.

"Anything else? Think hard."

Jack paused for further reflection. Then he raised his finger triumphantly.

"I remember now. One of them was chewing bubble-gum."

"Bubble-gum? You mean chewing-gum, don't you?"

"No, bubble-gum. He kept blowing bubbles. Pretty funny really, an old guy like that with kids' bubble-gum."

Stringer's jaw dropped. He sat back in the chair, and gazed at Jack in stupefaction.

"Which of them was it?" he breathed.

"The tall one," Jack said. "Quite a funny geezer, now I remember him."

Stringer put down his pen, and blinked in amazement. There was only one old man he knew who was tall, well-spoken and chewed bubble-gum. There *could* only be one such man.

"Well, fuck me," he said.

THIRTY-FOUR

"Is it, indeed?" Sybil said. "I see . . . Would you have the address by any chance . . . ? Yes, I'll hold . . . PO Box 5367, Al Rasheed Street, Baghdad . . . Yes, I'll take their telex number, if you have it . . . 213090. Thank you very much for your help. Goodbye."

She put down the phone and smiled. Things were going very nicely indeed. Sybil's first suspicion had been confirmed. Now it was a question of pursuing the new lead to its conclusion. To do this she needed the help of an old friend.

She popped her notes into her handbag, and went out into the hallway to put on her overcoat. Then she looked into the drawing-room, where Ogden & Co. were working on the latest instalment of the memoirs.

"How about another hired assassin?" Ogden suggested. "They're always guaranteed to liven things up."

"Good move," the Laird nodded. "Let's have a hunchback."

"Four feet tall, with a blood-curdling leer," added the Vicar. "And huge, powerful hands. Can kill his victims with one blow to the skull."

"A truly nasty piece of work," Beauchamp said enthusiastically. "Broken teeth, yellow skin—"

"Scabs," said the Vicar. "Syphilitic scabs."

"And a limp," Ogden said.

"Careful," the Laird warned. "We did a limping villain two weeks ago."

Ogden blew a brilliant pink gum-bubble, burst it, and nodded.

"Quite right," he conceded. "Mustn't debase the currency. Very well: why not give him a glass eye?"

"Better still," Beauchamp said, "no eye at all. Just a gaping socket . . ."

"I'm going out," Sybil announced. "I'll be taking the car."

"Cheerio, dear," the Vicar said absently. "You know, chaps, I think this hunchback should try to ravish some beautiful woman."

"A sex-fiend!" Ogden said brightly. "Now *that's* an idea . . ."

Sybil snorted contemptuously, and left the house. She had little use for one-eyed midget hunchbacked sex-fiends at the best of times, but now the proposition seemed especially trivial. Sybil had more important things to consider. She got in the car, and drove north.

Alison Wainwright had been a friend of Sybil's for over fifty years. They had both attended the same girls' boarding school, an establishment which prided itself on turning out ladies of strong character. But whereas Sybil had devoted her life to husband and home, Dr Wainwright had thrown herself into her studies, and took a university degree in chemistry. A Ph.D. soon followed, and this led to a research fellowship. But Dr Wainwright never attained the lofty heights of a professorial chair, and she eventually retired to a house in Hampstead, where her final years were being spent on a detailed study of witchcraft and mysticism.

Dr Wainwright had no difficulty in reconciling her scientific career with a passion for the occult. Her bookshelves sagged beneath the weight of countless mystical books and periodicals, and her walls were decorated with pentagrams and other arcane symbols. There was no furniture in her house, apart from a colourful collection of prayer mats. The remaining space was taken up by candelabras, joss-stick holders, and similar ritualistic bric-à-brac.

Dr Wainwright herself was a tall, red-haired lady who wore long flowery dresses and silken headscarves. In comparison with her friend she looked positively Bohemian, but Sybil was surprisingly respectful of Alison's passion for the transcendental.

"You're looking well," Sybil observed, as she struggled to make herself comfortable on a prayer mat.

"You too," Dr Wainwright smiled. "Have you been drinking that herbal tea I recommended? It does wonders for the blood."

"I wouldn't be a bit surprised," Sybil said. "I've been taking it regularly, and I'm sure it's been most beneficial."

In fact, Sybil had hesitated for some time before trying out the tea in question. But upon drinking her first cup, she found that the infusion looked and tasted like untreated sewage, and that was quite enough to convince Sybil of its medicinal worth.

"Anyway," Dr Wainwright said, "you told me on the phone that this was not just a social visit, and that you needed my help with something. I've spent the last two days trying to guess what it could be: an evil spirit in your house, perhaps? Has Godfrey been possessed by—"

"No," Sybil said hastily, "it's nothing like that. Actually, it's to do with chemistry."

Dr Wainwright's shoulders sagged in disappointment.

"Oh. *That*."

"I'm afraid so," Sybil said, and she took her papers out of her handbag. "Tell me: what's POC13?"

"Phosphorus oxychloride," Dr Wainwright said.

"Excellent," Sybil nodded."Just as I suspected."

"Is that all?"

"No, Alison, it's just the start. Let me explain."

Sybil gave a potted account of the abortive arms deal, the mysterious shipment—or non-shipment—on the SS *Flavio*, and Sybil's own latest theory on the subject. Dr Wainwright listened with mounting interest, and by the time Sybil had finished, her eyes were wide with excitement.

"Gosh," she said. "How intriguing!"

"Now you know why I need your help," Sybil said. "If you can tell me about some of the chemicals—what kind of thing they're normally used for—we might unravel the whole mystery."

"Possibly," Dr Wainwright said. "So, what are they?"

Sybil put on her glasses.

"I've told you about the phosphorus oxychloride: there were six tons of that. Then there were one hundred tons of thionyl chloride, two tons of potassium hydrogen fluoride, twenty tons of sodium cyanide, five tons of hydrogen fluoride, ten tons of phosphor, and one hundred and fifty tons of isopropyl alcohol. What do you think?"

Dr Wainwright rested her chin on her hands and puckered her lips.

"They're precursors," she said.

"What does that mean?"

"Precursors are simple base chemicals, used as the building

blocks for making complex products. There are heaps of them, and they're used in thousands of different processes."

"I see."

"And that's the problem," Dr Wainwright continued. "These chemicals could be used for just about anything."

"Pesticides?" Sybil said. "That's what it said on the Turkish shipping agent's note."

"It's possible, I suppose. To be honest, Sybil, I don't know anything about farming. There are some friends . . . but no, they're all organic farmers, so they wouldn't know either."

"Oh dear," Sybil sighed. "Just when I thought I was getting somewhere."

"Don't despair," Dr Wainwright said. "That combination does look a teeny-weeny bit familiar, and there is an old colleague who can check it for me. He's a charming fellow called Heinz Erler, who used to work at my university. You'll love him."

"I'm sure," Sybil said drily. "And he might be able to tell us how these—these precursors were going to be used?"

"Perhaps," Dr Wainwright said. "He's worked in lots of different branches of chemistry, and he's got a mind like a library."

"Very well. Let's ask him."

"Will do, Sybil. Now, have I told you about my latest book? It's a critique of Nostradamus' prophecies, and I've written it from a Zen viewpoint. You'd love it."

THIRTY-FIVE

Colonel Kyle banged hard on the Laird's front door.

"Fergus Buchanan," he called.

There was no reply. The colonel banged harder and raised his voice.

"Fergus Buchanan! Come forth!"

But the Laird did not come forth. Colonel Kyle began to kick the door, but to no avail. It was a stout, oaken door, and the colonel's shoes had little effect upon it. More importantly, they had no effect on the Laird, who was clearly not at home.

"Fergus Buchanan!" Colonel Kyle bawled. "Come unto me!"

The front door of the adjoining house opened, and a little old lady popped her head out.

"Good morning," she said brightly. "Are you looking for Mr Buchanan? I think he's with Mr Ogden and the others."

"Ogden?"

"Yes, Clive Ogden. They usually go to Mr Croft's house."

"Mr Croft," the colonel repeated thoughtfully.

These names were new to him, but they were clearly of significance.

"They're all good friends," the old lady said. "They seem to do everything together, nowadays. Quite inseparable, really."

She smiled wistfully.

"That Mr Ogden's such a card," she giggled. "Always making jokes. Mr Beauchamp's nice, too. He used to be in antiques. In fact, they'll all very nice."

"As it says in the psalm, 'they are all alike depraved,'" Colonel Kyle replied. "'There is none that does good, no, not one.'"

"Well, you're entitled to your opinion," the old lady said, "but they've always been very polite to me. Give people a chance, I say."

Colonel Kyle grunted. Giving people a chance was not really his style.

"Have you had a dispute with them?" the old lady asked. "Is that why you're trying to find them?"

"The strong lion perishes for lack of prey," Colonel Kyle explained.

"They're very reasonable people," the old lady said. "If you're upset with them about something, I'm sure they'll be only too happy to sort it out like gentlemen."

"Gentlemen," Colonel Kyle sneered. "Pah."

"If you like," she offered, "I can give you Mr Croft's phone number. As I say, they're usually at his house, working on Mr Ogden's memoirs."

The colonel took out a pad and pencil, and gazed at her expectantly.

"One moment," she said, and she popped indoors. A few seconds later she reappeared holding a telephone directory.

"Here you are: Godfrey Croft. Though the others call him Vicar, for some reason. A joke, I suppose. They really are a cheery lot!"

But the humour was wasted on Colonel Kyle. He wrote down the address and phone number, and gave a curt nod.

"The Lord be with you," he said.

"Goodbye," the old lady smiled. "I hope you sort out your problem with them. There are few disputes you can't settle amicably, are there?"

The colonel gave another grunt, and walked away. Despite the old lady's optimism, an amicable settlement was not on the cards. The colonel had something else in mind—something more in keeping with his taste for Old Testament cataclysms.

THIRTY-SIX

"Keep going," urged the Laird.

"Don't stop," said the Vicar.

Ogden gave a muffled grunt of acknowledgment. He was giving his friends a practical demonstration of the virtues of American bubble-gum. The emission from his lips was a technicolour monstrosity, almost as big as Ogden's head. The bubble swirled with lurid greens, reds, yellows and purples, and showed no sign of collapsing as Ogden paused to breathe in more air through his nose.

"That's it," said the Laird. "One more puff—oh, Lord!"

Without warning the bubble burst, and left a polychromatic mask plastered across Ogden's features.

"Damn," Ogden muttered, as his friends roared with laughter. "Anyway, you take my point. There isn't a sweet-shop in London that sells anything this powerful."

"It's a good thing you don't have a beard," the Vicar observed.

"True," Ogden nodded, as he peeled the sticky mess off his face. "Though some of it's got into my hair. Blast."

"One has to suffer for one's art," the Laird sympathised. "Pity Jeremy wasn't here to see it."

"Where is he?" Ogden inquired.

"Heaven knows," the Laird shrugged. "He told me he was going away for a couple of days, but he wouldn't say where."

"Really?" the Vicar said curiously. "It's not like Jeremy to be so secretive."

"Must have caught the bug from Sybil," Ogden said. "She's been pretty cagey, of late. Any idea what your scrumptious wife's been up to, Vicar?"

"None," the Vicar admitted. "But I'm not complaining. It's been jolly peaceful here for the last few days."

"Perhaps she's got a lover," the Laird suggested.

The Vicar grimaced in disgust.

"I hardly think so," he said. "What sort of chap would want to—you know, with Sybil? Seems rather far-fetched."

"Oh, I don't know," Ogden mused. "There are lots of men who are jolly keen on discipline. The head-shrinkers say it's all a throwback to school: cold showers, regular floggings, and all that."

The Vicar gave a perplexed shrug.

"No accounting for taste, I suppose."

"I've got it," Ogden grinned. "She's run off with Jeremy, and they're going to set up a love-nest in the Outer Hebrides, flogging antiques to the sheep-farmers."

"Interesting theory," the Vicar nodded. "I'd miss Jeremy, though."

"Well, wherever he is, I hope he's back by next week," the Laird said. "He really ought to be here for the launching of the book."

"Absolutely," Ogden agreed. "I mean, it's not every book that's banned before it's written, much less published."

The book in question was, of course, the collected memoirs of Clive Ogden, which were to be published in the United States under the title *The Ogden Papers*. As expected, the Government had banned their sale in the United Kingdom. But the American publishers had received so many advance mail-orders from Britain that the book was guaranteed to be the country's first illicit number-one bestseller.

Of course, Ogden & Co. had not stopped writing the memoirs. The *Baltimore Bugle* was still running fresh instalments each week, and would continue to do so until international interest had subsided. There was even talk of a second volume of *The Ogden Papers*, or "Son of Ogden", as the Laird put it.

Given the excitement surrounding the new publication, the inquiry into the missing arms-shipment had taken a back seat recently, though Ogden and his friends were not giving up on it. As expected, Mr Blake was not satisfied with the Vicar's theory about what had happened, and he was keen that the matter be pursued further.

"It's all a question of finding a fresh angle," Ogden said. "I keep thinking I've overlooked something. In fact, I had that feeling before I came home from the States. Something obvious I haven't thought of. Perhaps—"

155

He was interrupted by a ring of the telephone. The Vicar went over to answer it.

"Hello? Godfrey Croft speaking."

The man at the other end spoke in a low hiss: "He who walks in integrity walks securely. But he who perverts his ways will be found out."

The Vicar held out the phone receiver.

"I think it's for you, Clive."

"Really?" Ogden said. "Who is it?"

"He didn't say."

Ogden shrugged and took the phone.

"Hello?"

"There shall be blood throughout all the land of Egypt," the voice said, "both in vessels of wood and vessels of stone."

"You don't say?" Ogden replied calmly. "Thanks for the tip. But there's nothing to worry about: I wasn't planning to take a holiday there. Who's speaking, by the way?"

Whatever reaction the other man expected from Ogden, this was certainly not it. The man snorted, and complained: "As the psalm says, 'Fools, when will you be wise?'"

"Probably never, in my case," Ogden admitted. "What exactly were you after, old man?"

"Avenge the people of Israel on the Midianites, sayeth the Lord. Execute the Lord's vengeance on Midian."

Ogden blinked curiously. Then he snapped his fingers and grinned.

"I've got it," he said. "You're selling double-glazing, aren't you? Or is it fitted kitchens? You chaps are always thinking up new ways of flogging your products. Quite a good idea, really: target the religious types. Well, I'm sorry to say—"

"It is written in the Book of Deuteronomy: 'you shall be driven mad by the sight your eyes shall see.'"

"I'm sure I would," Ogden chuckled. "I bet it's a real humdinger of a fitted kitchen. But the fact is, old chap, I don't actually *need* one at the moment."

The man at the other end was growing restless. This conversation was not going the way he had planned.

"'You shall break them with a rod of iron,' sayeth the Lord," he screamed, "'and dash them in pieces like a potter's vessel.'"

"My word," Ogden exclaimed. "The hard sell, what?"

"Watch, therefore, for you know neither the day nor the hour."

"I'll do that," Ogden promised. "What did you say your name was? Deuteronomy Double-Glazing? Jeremiah Fitted Kitchens? Hello? Hello? Oh dear, he's rung off."

"Who was it?" the Laird asked.

"A salesman, I think. Has a hilarious new way of hawking his goods: plenty of Old Testament blood and thunder."

"What was he selling?"

"Not too sure," Ogden said. "It's an interesting sales technique, but it needs a little refinement. Anyway, what was I saying . . . ?"

THIRTY-SEVEN

"I'm sorry I'm late," Sybil said. "The man at the newspaper-cutting agency took longer than I expected."

"That's all right," Dr Wainwright said. "Meet Professor Heinz Erler."

Sybil shook hands with a shrivelled old man who had no hair, no eyebrows, and no discernible sense of humour.

"Charmed," he said gloomily.

"Heinz is an old friend of mine," Dr Wainwright explained. "He thinks he knows what those chemicals were for, don't you Heinz?"

The professor nodded unhappily.

"Oh yes," he said. "I have seen this combination of precursors before. Dr Wainwright did not tell me where you found them, but I can guess."

"Can you?" Sybil asked, in surprise.

"Oh yes. There are vast rewards to be made from human misery. I presume you have found one more company whose shareholders are thriving on the profits of pain and death."

Sybil glanced uneasily at Dr Wainwright. The Vicar's wife disliked frivolity, and she approved of people with a sober, unsmiling approach to life. But even Sybil had her limits, and Professor Erler was perhaps a little too mournful to be taken entirely seriously.

"Do you know anything at all about this subject, Mrs Croft?" he asked.

"I'm afraid not," Sybil admitted.

"So," the Professor said. "I will explain. Sit and listen."

They sat down on Dr Wainwright's prayer rugs, and Professor Erler began his story.

"As you will know, the first chemical weapon was mustard gas. This was used in the First World War, yes?"

"I know," Sybil said. "My father was struck down by it. He never fully recovered."

"Just so. It is a simple thing to manufacture: you take thiodiglycol and add spirits of salt. The results are terrible."

One of the professor's eyes screwed half-shut, and he tilted his head back slightly.

"Terrible," he repeated. "When it first touches the skin, it feels like cold water, and smells awful. It creates large, agonising blisters. If breathed in, it attacks the respiratory system. Then it attacks the bone marrow, and produces anaemia, yes? This usually leads to death. A horrible, slow, lingering death."

There was a faint note of morbid satisfaction in the professor's tone, and he almost smiled. Then he raised one skeletal finger in a gesture of caution.

"But death cannot be guaranteed."

"Can't it?" Sybil stammered.

"Oh no. So mustard gas is primarily used as an incapacitating agent, yes? It is a crude weapon. In the history of chemical warfare, mustard gas belongs with the bows and the arrows."

"I see," Sybil nodded.

"So," the professor continued, "after the First World War, the great powers began to look for better weapons. And the Nazis found them. They discovered—nerve agents!"

He paused for dramatic effect.

"What are they?" Sybil asked.

"The ultimate chemical weapon, Mrs Croft," the professor said. "Nerve agents are ten times more lethal than mustard gas. And *thickened* nerve agents are better still. They are clear, colourless, like glue. They cling to the skin, yes? Minute amounts are needed to kill. Minute amounts, Mrs Croft."

"Is—is that so?"

"Oh yes," the professor nodded. "One tiny drop—a sugar-lump dose—will kill three thousand people. It will kill them immediately upon contact with the skin. And it will kill them horribly."

His head tilted back, and his eye screwed shut once more.

"Their limbs vibrate uncontrollably," he said. "There is copious vomiting and defaecation. Finally, Mrs Croft, there is suffocation."

Dr Wainwright grinned feebly.

"How jolly," she said.

"As I say, the Nazis first found them. There were two kinds:

159

Tabun and Sarin. But the formulas were simple. So childishly simple that they assumed their enemies must also have them, yes? This is why they were never used."

"Did we have them?" Sybil asked.

"Oh no," Professor Erler said. "But the Nazis never found out, God be thanked. Then, after the war, the formulas were patented. They were freely available in journals everywhere. Now, any idiot can make them."

Sybil pointed to her list.

"And that's what those chemicals were for?"

"It is quite possible," the professor nodded. "These precursors can be used harmlessly, of course. But taken together, it is another matter: the thionyl chloride, the potassium hydrogen fluoride, the sodium cyanide, the hydrogen fluoride, the phosphor and the alcohol: with these one can make Sarin. And with the phosphorus oxychloride, one can also make Tabun."

Sybil wrote this down.

"What about the processing equipment?" she asked. "Is that very elaborate?"

"Oh no. Very simple, Mrs Croft. Some reactor vessels, piping and centrifuges. They must be made of a special alloy, because these chemicals are highly corrosive, yes? But it is all easily available."

"Aren't chemical weapons illegal?" Dr Wainwright said.

Professor Erler shook his head.

"There is only one international agreement," he said. "The Geneva Protocol of 1925. But do people observe this? I think not. And officially, only three countries have these weapons: the United States, the Soviet Union and France. They all claim their chemicals would only be used in retaliation, but who can be sure? And many other countries are known to have them also: Syria, Korea, Burma, Taiwan, Libya, Iran, Iraq, Afghanistan, Ethiopia, China, Chile—these are just a few, yes?"

"But aren't there any controls?"

"Oh yes," the professor said. "The United States and the EEC countries have banned the export of key precursors to certain countries, for this reason. There is watch-list of certain nations who are known to make nerve gases and nerve agents. There are fines and other penalties for those who export to these nations."

"How well is all this enforced?" Sybil asked.

160

The professor spread his hands apart.

"They do what they can, yes? People have been fined. But how do you police an industry so large, Mrs Croft? There are over nine thousand different chemicals. The world trade is worth one hundred and fifty *billion* US dollars every year, yes?"

"Which countries are on the watch-list you mentioned?"

"All the ones I named," the professor replied. "Many of them have responded by manufacturing their own precursors. It is not difficult to do. But they will always welcome ready-made precursors from Europe and the United States, yes?"

Sybil put away her note-book and smiled.

"Well, I think that's all I needed to know," she said. "Thank you very much, Professor."

"Pleasure," he replied miserably. "I hope this is of use to whatever work you are engaged upon."

"It is," Sybil said. "In fact, I think a big question has just been answered."

"Glad to hear it," Dr Wainwright said. "Now, let's talk about something less gloomy, shall we? I've just been reading the most marvellous book on Tibetan burial rites . . ."

THIRTY-EIGHT

"It's Ogden," Stringer said. "It has to be."

"Can you prove it?" asked the D-G.

"Of course I can," Stringer grinned. "How many old men do you know who chew bubble-gum?"

"Not many," the D-G admitted. "But—"

"And the other one had a limp. I've checked Godfrey Croft's file: he had a hip replacement recently."

"Indeed. But—"

"Croft worked in 'A' Directorate. He knows all about phone-taps, bugs, you name it. It was his speciality."

"That's very good," the D-G conceded. "But I'm not sure if it's enough."

"There's no need to speculate," Stringer said. "Let's hand this stuff over to the legal department, and see what they think."

"If you like," the D-G nodded. "But I'll be surprised if they disagree with me."

"Why?" Stringer demanded.

"If it were an ordinary prosecution, your evidence would probably be good enough to secure a conviction. But under these circumstances, we'd almost certainly lose. Ogden's too famous now, and everybody knows we're out to punish him for those memoirs."

"But the old bastard's broken the law," Stringer protested.

"Says who?" the D-G smiled. "Ogden's lawyer would claim we fabricated the evidence. It was our tap, wasn't it? He'll say we switched it on purpose."

Stringer slumped back in his chair.

"For Christ's sake," he complained. "What do I have to do to nick that bastard? Sleep with him, or something? If we can't arrest Ogden on the evidence I've got, then we might as well pack up and piss off home."

"Relax," the D-G advised. "We just need one more piece of evidence, but it must be of the right kind."

"Yeah," Stringer said bitterly. "Written in fucking tablets of stone. And there's no such thing, is there?"

"It must be something that has no connection with us, so we can't be accused of rigging the evidence. Ogden and his friends must be implicated by something *they* have said or done."

"Apart from the tap, you mean?"

"Exactly. After all, they couldn't have carried out the switch without advance preparation."

"Don't be too sure," Stringer said. "From what that guy Kevin tells me, a five year old could change the wiring on the frame. All you need is a screwdriver."

"Are you telling me they did it on the spur of the moment?" the D-G said incredulously. "They just strolled into the exchange and—"

"I wouldn't put it past them. You know what Ogden's like: he probably had a couple of drinks, and decided it would be a real giggle to mess around with one of our taps. Crazy old twat."

"I can't believe it," the D-G said. "There must have been some planning. What about the ID card Croft waved at the engineer?"

"It was probably his pension book," Stringer said. "Goodhart didn't bother to read it."

"Oh really," the D-G winced.

"I know, I know," Stringer sighed. "I chewed the guy's ear off about it, for all the good that'll do. You know what the stupid berk said to me? He knew they were kosher because they drove up in the right kind of van. Of all the dumb, shit-brained—wait a minute . . ."

"A van, you say?"

"Yeah," Stringer nodded eagerly. "That's what he said. They came in one of the Reserve vans, just like the previous lot. That's it!"

"Locate that van," the D-G said, "and we'll have our evidence."

"They couldn't talk their way out of that one," Stringer agreed. "In fact, we'd have them by the short and curlies."

"Find that van," the D-G commanded.

"Definitely. I'll need Special Branch help, of course."

The D-G grimaced.

"How much help?"

"I can't be sure," Stringer said. "Have you any idea how many

163

old Telecom vans are sold second-hand? It must run to thousands. And if Ogden's been smart, he'll have bought his from someone well outside the Greater London area. It'll need a lot of manpower to trace it."

The D-G frowned uneasily. Matters of economy were never far from his thoughts.

"Never mind," he decided. "Get whatever the job needs. If we're going to make an example of Ogden, we'd better do things properly."

Stringer beamed in satisfaction.

"I couldn't agree with you more," he said.

THIRTY-NINE

"Jeremy!" the Vicar said, with mild surprise. "Where are you phoning from?"

"Holland."

"Good heavens. What are you doing there?"

"Never mind," Beauchamp said. "I've unearthed something important. Mrs Lemiers was looking through her husband's things, and she found a small book in the breast-pocket of one of his jackets. It's full of phone numbers. One of them was for a man called Pete Michener—"

"Never heard of him," the Vicar said.

"I know you haven't," Beauchamp said irritably. "I checked his number: it's the same one as Magnum Incorporated's."

"Gosh," said the Vicar. "That's smart work, Jeremy."

"I thought so too," Beauchamp agreed. "It means my Lemiers is back in the running. So tell the others, will you? I'll be catching a flight home tomorrow morning, and I'll be around after lunch, all right?"

"Yes, of course. Congratulations, old man."

"Cheerio."

The Vicar put the phone down, and gave the news to his friends.

"Good old Jeremy," the Laird said. "Just when things were beginning to dry up, as well."

"You realise what this means?" Ogden said. "We've now got a firm link between Lemiers and that fellow Kyle."

"Kyle's company, at least."

"Of course you have," Sybil said, as she came into the room. "You always had it, but you were too jolly incompetent to see it."

"Good afternoon, O radiant one," Ogden said. "Have you come to cast some shafts of golden sunlight upon the proceedings?"

"Someone ought to," Sybil sniffed.

She put down her handbag and took a seat.

"Your big mistake," she said, "was to keep looking for a shipment of arms. You see, there never were any."

The men glanced at each other inquiringly.

"Do you know what she's talking about?" the Vicar asked the Laird.

"Haven't the foggiest," the Laird admitted.

"She's your wife, Vicar," Ogden observed. "If you can't make sense of her, what can we do?"

Sybil shook her head contemptuously.

"If you'd spent more time thinking, and less on making silly jokes, you might have solved this puzzle. As it is, I've done it for you."

The Vicar thoughtfully scratched his jaw.

"You're saying that Jeremy's Lemiers is the one we want?"

"That's right."

"But until now, you've been saying the exact opposite. And you tore a strip off Jeremy for going to see his widow."

"That was earlier," Sybil said dismissively. "I didn't know her husband was illegally exporting chemicals, did I?"

"*What?*"

"Start at the beginning," Ogden suggested. "Nice and slowly, and preferably in words of one syllable."

"As one would treat an imbecile," Sybil nodded. "Don't worry, Clive, I know how to teach you things."

She produced her notes, put on her glasses, and began her story.

"There were two clues in Lemiers' papers, and you missed both of them. The first was the name SEPP, and the accompanying address: PO Box 5367. The second was the order next to it: two more tons of POCl3.

"SEPP is not a name. It stands for the State Establishment for Pesticide Production, in Iraq. And POCl3 is the standard symbol for phosphorus oxychloride.

"If you recall, the Turkish shipping agent's receipt mentioned, among other things, sixty tons of phosphorus oxychloride. This was destined for the State Organisation for Chemical Industries in Baghdad, Iraq. SEPP is a subdivision of this organisation, and they can both be reached at PO Box 5367, Al Rasheed Street, Baghdad, Iraq."

Ogden clapped his hands.

"Full marks, Sybil. Is that it?"

"By no means," Sybil said. "SEPP is also the government department responsible for Iraq's chemical-warfare project."

"You don't say?"

Sybil took out the newspaper cuttings she had bought from the agency.

"Apparently, there's a big production plant about forty kilometres south of a place called Samarra. It says here that the plant makes at least a thousand tons of chemical weapons per year. Of course, the Iraqis claim it's a pesticide plant. But they don't have any kind of pesticide industry, and there's no doubt about the real purpose of this factory."

The Laird raised his pipe in an inquiring gesture.

"Okay," he said. "But if the *Flavio* was taking chemicals for Iraq, why did Carter think it was taking arms for the United States?"

"Because that's what he was supposed to think," Sybil said. "It was Lemiers who organised the shipment, claiming to be Carter on the phone."

"That was my theory," the Vicar protested. "And you said it was nonsense."

"I'll admit you were right about that, Godfrey," Sybil said magnanimously. "But that's just about all. Anyway, the Naples authorities checked the boat before it left, and found no guns. That was because there were never any. The only thing that was wrong about this shipment of chemicals was its final destination: Iraq. You see, under United States and European law, we're not allowed to sell them chemicals which can be used to make weapons. And these particular chemicals are used in the manufacture of two nerve agents, Sarin and Tabun."

"Are you sure about that?" Ogden asked.

"Of course I'm sure," Sybil snapped. "What do you think I've been doing for the last couple of days? I've sought expert opinions on every part of—"

"All right, all right," Ogden chuckled. "Forgive my impudence."

"Wait a minute," the Laird said. "If it's illegal to send this stuff to Iraq, why didn't the authorities stop it in Naples?"

"Because they didn't know where it was going," Sybil replied. "The goods were marked down for a shipping agent in Turkey.

There was nothing on Captain Salvucci's export documents to suggest that they would then go to Iraq. In fact, even the captain didn't know where they would end up, until the Turkish agent gave him his receipt."

"Fair enough," the Laird said. "But you still haven't explained why Carter thought he was shipping arms."

"It's quite simple," Sybil said. "The original deal was between Lemiers and the American company, Magnum Inc. The Americans gave Lemiers all the information and support he needed to pose as an international arms dealer, and that's why Carter believed he was genuine. But the point of the exercise was to sell chemicals to the Iraqis, in violation of international law. Remember, chemical weapons played a big part in the Gulf War."

"But that's all over," the Vicar observed.

"Yes, and why was it brought to an end? Iran had overwhelming superiority in numbers, remember. But the Iraqis overcame that problem by using chemical weapons. And apart from the fighting on the battlefield, these weapons were used in reprisal attacks on villages. They wiped out five thousand people in their own town of Halabja for not resisting Iranian occupation.

"Besides, there's always the chance that hostilities will re-open. If so, Iraq wants to be ready with Sarin and Tabun. And the Iraqis haven't just used these nerve agents against Iranians: they're still having trouble with Kurdish insurgents, and they're using chemical weapons to sort out that problem, too."

Ogden was still not convinced.

"But why does the CIA want to peddle chemicals to the Iraqis, if it's against their own country's law?"

"The law didn't stop them selling arms to Iranians," Sybil observed. "And it's the Iraqis who the Americans have always supported, isn't it? Anyway, I didn't think the CIA were ever particularly troubled by laws."

"True," said the Vicar. "But if this Colonel Kyle wanted to sell chemicals to the Iraqis, why didn't he just pay Lemiers to send them? Why did he bring Carter into it, and swindle him?"

"That was the clever bit," Sybil said. "Suppose something had gone terribly wrong with this shipment. For instance, a snap inspection by somebody in authority, who was also prepared to question the Turkish shipping agent. If that had happened, there would have been nothing to link the cargo of chemicals with

Magnum Inc. and the CIA. After all, the ship was ordered by an Englishman called Carter."

"What if Carter had pointed the finger at Colonel Kyle?"

"Why should he? Kyle had ordered arms, not chemicals. And even if Kyle were questioned, nothing could be pinned on him. He would claim he'd never heard of anyone called Lemiers, and there'd be no evidence to connect the two men. He'd show the investigators Magnum Inc.'s account books, which would prove that all his dealings were with reputable, legitimate arms dealers. Furthermore, he hadn't sought out Carter—Carter had been introduced to him."

"And as we know," Ogden observed, "when the cargo went 'missing', Carter was not in a position to complain to the authorities, because he thought he'd been organising a dodgy arms deal. Splendid, Sybil. You've done a magnificent job."

"Hear, hear," said the Laird.

"Yes, you have done quite well," the Vicar agreed.

"Quite well?" Sybil boomed. "Quite well? I've done superbly well, Godfrey. I've solved the whole mystery."

"Not quite," the Vicar grinned. "You still haven't explained why Carter was murdered, along with the others, and who was responsible."

Sybil paused. Her husband had clearly scored a point.

"It's the same problem I had," the Vicar sympathised. "You see, these things are never entirely straightforward, are they?"

"Well, I can't be expected to think of *everything*," Sybil said.

"Of course you can't," Ogden smiled. "But don't worry. I think we might be able to clear up that little problem as well. You see, I don't think the CIA really did want to sell chemicals to the Iraqis. Let's just think this through, shall we?"

FORTY

"Try harder," Stringer said.

"That's all I know," Blewitt insisted. "They were just four old blokes. You know: wrinkles, white hair, the usual stuff. What more do you want?"

"Names," Stringer said.

Mr Blewitt shook his head.

"I do cars," he said, "not christenings."

"How did they pay?"

"Cash, as I recall. Hang on."

He looked in his account book and nodded.

"Yeah, cash."

"And you're sure it was this registration number?" Stringer said.

"Positive. I keep records, don't I?"

Stringer glanced at his colleague, a burly gentleman from the Special Branch who was holding a walkie-talkie.

"What do you think, Ted?"

The Special Branch man shrugged.

"Could be them. I've checked the registration number with the Telecom records: the van concerned was never used by the Reserve fleet. But Croft had to re-paint the logo anyway, so he probably just added the Reserve code himself."

"Yeah," Stringer said. "Are your people going to take much longer?"

"Another five minutes," Ted said. "They're moving as fast as they can."

Stringer guessed that the van had been re-sold immediately after Ogden and the Vicar had visited the exchange. His investigation team had obtained a list of vans that had come on to the market through private hands, and this was now being cross-checked with the number Mr Blewitt had provided. With luck, this would provide two sets of identifications, and both would point to Ogden.

170

"Right," Stringer said. "If that's all you can remember, Mr Blewitt, try these for size."

He took out a set of photographs and gave them to the car dealer.

"No," Mr Blewitt said, as he saw the first photo. "Nor this one. No. No. Hang on a minute . . ."

He peered intently at the fifth photo, and nodded slowly.

"Yeah, he was one of them. Had a wig, now I remember. One of the worst ones I've ever seen."

"Keep going."

"No. No. Here's another one. Tall guy. Posh accent. They all had posh voices, now I think about it."

"Good," Stringer said. "Do you remember anything else about this one. Anything unusual?"

Mr Blewitt scratched his head.

"Yeah, I do. He chewed gum. Bubble-gum."

"Did he indeed?" Stringer grinned. "Look through the rest of the photos, will you?"

The Special branch officer's walkie-talkie crackled into life, and a female voice inquired: "Alpha Four?"

"Alpha Four," Ted replied. "What have you got?"

"A dealer in Bracknell. We've just phoned him: says he bought the van from two old men. Out of date tax disc, apparently."

"Nice one," Ted said. "Let's have the details."

"That makes sense," Stringer said, as Ted wrote down the dealer's name and address. "If they only wanted it for a couple of days, they wouldn't have bothered to get it taxed."

"These two," Mr Blewitt announced, holding up another pair of photographs. "The one on the left paid the money."

Stringer took the four photographs and held them together.

"Beauchamp, Ogden, Croft and Buchanan. Lovely."

"You been looking for them?" Mr Blewitt said.

"Oh yes," Stringer said quietly. "We've been looking for them, all right."

"They don't look like villains to me."

"Believe me, Mr Blewitt, these are four bad lads. Don't be fooled by their age and the endearing little grins on their faces. These old fuckers belong inside, and I'm going to enjoy putting them there."

Mr Blewitt looked sceptical.

"What have they done?"

"You wouldn't believe me if I told you," Stringer sighed. "Anyway, thanks for your help, Mr Blewitt. There'll be somebody round this afternoon to take a full statement from you, and you may have to appear in court as a witness."

"Okay," Ted said, as he put away his note-book. "Over to Bracknell, I suppose."

"Definitely," Stringer nodded. "Then you can pick up a warrant for their arrest. By Christ, Ted, I'm looking forward to this."

FORTY-ONE

"Is that you, Chester?" Ogden asked.

"Yes," said a high-pitched American voice. "Hello, Clive. How are things?"

"Fine," Ogden said. "Listen, I'm in a call-box, and I don't have much change. Did you get my letter?"

"Yes I did, Clive. It's deliciously mysterious. What does it all *mean*?"

"It's just as I explained in the letter," Ogden said. "The inner envelope contains something that might save my neck if things go wrong around here."

"Why can't I read it?" Chester demanded. "Don't you trust me, or something?"

"I trust you implicitly, old man. But if you don't read it, you can't be incriminated in any way, see?"

"Okay," Chester said reluctantly. "But I want the *full* story when you're next over here."

"You'll get it," Ogden promised. "Now, do you remember what to do?"

"Sure. If anything happens, I'll hear from your lawyer. Then I'll take the envelope to Mr Stompfweiner in Baltimore."

"Good man," Ogden said. "Any questions?"

"No," Chester said. "Except what the *hell* is going on?"

"Wait and see," Ogden grinned. "Speak to you soon."

"Bye, Clive."

Ogden put the phone down and left the call-box. He assumed that his own phone was being tapped, and although international calls were also monitored, the chances of his being overheard were greatly diminished. He popped a stick of bubble-gum into his mouth, and walked back to the Vicar's house.

The Laird, Beauchamp and the Vicar were in the drawing-room, putting the finishing touches to the latest instalment of the memoir.

"Leave it hanging," the Vicar suggested. "After all, Clive's just about to lead a frontal assult on the villain's HQ. He doesn't really know what to expect there—"

"Apart from a lot of trouble," Beauchamp said.

"Exactly," the Laird nodded. "So let's keep the readers guessing, and save up the fireworks for the next episode."

"Very well," said the Vicar. "We'll do that. It all works reasonably neatly, doesn't it?"

He typed out the last sentence, and drew the page out of the typewriter. A quick glance at the script ensured that there were no spelling errors, and he handed the instalment to Beauchamp.

"Off you go," he said.

Beauchamp stood up and put on his jacket.

"Why the rush?" Ogden asked, as he entered the room.

"Mr Stompfweiner phoned while you were out," the Laird explained. "He's going to run this instalment one day early, because there's a national holiday or something. Anyway, he wants it in tonight."

"There's a fax bureau about half a mile from here," Beauchamp said, "and I picked the short straw."

"Why don't you take our car?" the Vicar suggested.

"He can't," Sybil called out from the kitchen. "The insurance doesn't cover him."

"In that case, Sybil, why don't you drive him over?" the Laird said.

"I'm much too busy," Sybil said briskly.

The Vicar grinned, and put his finger to his lips. Then he reached over to the table, and handed Beauchamp the car keys. Beauchamp nodded appreciatively.

"Never mind," he said loudly. "I shan't be long."

He folded up the papers, slipped them into his jacket, and went out.

"Chester got the letter, all right?" the Vicar inquired.

"He did," Ogden said. "The old darling was almost wetting himself with inquisitiveness about the inner envelope. Still, Chester's a reliable sort. By the way, have you phoned Mr Blake yet?"

"Beauchamp did. Obviously, it was a guarded conversation, but Blake made it clear that he supports our theory entirely."

"I should hope so too," Ogden said. "After all the work we've done."

"Anyway," said the Vicar, "what's our next move?"

"Well," Ogden said thoughtfully, "I've been mulling over this one, and it occurs to me that—"

He was interrupted by the front-door bell.

"Who could that be?" the Vicar wondered.

"Are you going to answer it?" Sybil called out.

"No," the Laird replied nastily. "We're much too busy."

"For heaven's sake," Sybil groaned.

The others heard her stomp impatiently to the front door.

"Yes?" she asked.

Whoever it was did not reply. The men could hear a strange, feminine gurgling sound.

"What on earth's that?" Ogden said.

"Better take a look," the Laird suggested.

As he got to his feet, Sybil was propelled into the drawing-room with considerable force. She crashed into the Laird, and they were both sent sprawling across the carpet. In the doorway stood a large, angry American gentleman, who said in a thunderous voice: "Enter into the rock and hide in the dust from before the terror of the Lord!"

"By George!" Ogden exclaimed. "It's the double-glazing salesman."

"He's insane," Sybil gasped, as she picked herself up off the floor. "Utterly mad!"

The Vicar nodded thoughtfully.

"Colonel Kyle, I presume?"

This greeting did not improve the colonel's humour. His fists clenched tightly, and several large veins bulged in his forehead.

"The shatterer has come up against you!" he bawled. "Man the ramparts! Watch the road! Gird up your loins!"

"All at once?" Ogden said.

"Careful, Clive," the Laird warned. "This chap's completely off his rocker."

"The thought had crossed my mind," Ogden admitted. "Not exactly a model of restraint, is he?"

"But now they make sport of me," Colonel Kyle snarled. "Behold, you scoffers, and wonder, and perish; for I do a deed in your days, a deed you will never believe, if one declares it to you."

175

"Of course you do," the Vicar said soothingly. "I'm sure you're a very enterprising fellow."

"Perish?" the Laird repeated. "Did he say 'perish'?"

"I'm afraid so," Ogden said, and he blew a large gum-bubble.

"Oh really, Clive!" Sybil snapped. "Aren't you going to do something?"

"What do you suggest?" Ogden retorted. "I left my sub-machine-gun at home this morning."

Colonel Kyle's lip curled in disdain.

"They are a perverse and crooked generation," he observed. "You serpents, you brood of vipers! How are you to escape being sentenced to hell?"

"We had a reasonable chance, until you popped in," the Vicar replied.

"Hear this, you aged men!" the colonel yelled. "Which of you is called Fergus Buchanan?"

"What?" the Laird blinked.

"Fergus Buchanan," the colonel repeated.

Suddenly, Ogden had a bright idea.

"He's gone out," he said quickly. "We're expecting him back soon."

The colonel nodded grimly, and drew out a pistol.

"The time is near," he said. "For the great day of wrath has come, and who can stand before it?"

FORTY-TWO

Beauchamp stopped the car outside the Vicar's house and swore. Some character had taken his parking space, and Beauchamp had to find somewhere else. This meant that Sybil would realise that he had borrowed the car, and there would be further consternation in the Croft household.

"Damn," he muttered. "And it was all going so well."

The instalment was now in the hands of the *Baltimore Bugle*, and he had been looking forward to a clear afternoon of tea and chatter in the Vicar's drawing-room. But Sybil's forthcoming tantrum would put paid to that.

There was another space about twenty yards up the road. To reach it, Beauchamp had to pass the Vicar's front door. As he did so, he noticed a most peculiar spectacle in the drawing-room. In fact, it was so extraordinary that Beauchamp was convinced his eyes were playing tricks on him. He braked, and reversed the car so he could take another look.

Beauchamp had not seen a mirage. There really was a man standing in the doorway with a gun in his hand. And to judge from the expressions on the faces of Ogden, the Vicar, Sybil and the Laird, they were not being shown the latest brand of water-pistol. The gunman seemed deeply upset about something, and the others were not managing to calm him down.

"Crumbs," Beauchamp muttered. "Better fetch the police."

He put his foot down on the accelerator and sped away.

As time passed in the drawing-room, Colonel Kyle was growing restless. Matters were not helped by Sybil, who insisted on telling the colonel precisely what she thought of him.

"You're a disgrace to your country," she said. "You know perfectly well that it was against the law to sell those chemicals to the Iraqis."

The colonel was not impressed.

177

"Does it not say in the letter of Paul to the Galatians: 'all who rely on works of law are under a curse'?"

"Love, fifteen," Ogden grinned.

"Besides," Sybil said, "if you were a religious man, you'd never have done any of those terrible things. Just think, an entire city could be wiped out by those chemicals you sent. That doesn't sound very religious to me."

"Fifteen all," Ogden said.

Colonel Kyle shrugged indifferently.

"Does evil befall a city, unless the Lord has done it?" he quoted.

"That's right," Sybil said heavily. "Put the blame on God. Very responsible, I must say. And I can promise you, colonel, the Church of England's God doesn't put up with that sort of thing."

"Read the words in Deuteronomy, woman," Colonel Kyle advised. "'The Lord your God is a devouring fire, a jealous God.'"

"Fifteen, thirty," Ogden said.

"Oh well," Sybil said dismissively. "You can prove anything with scripture, I suppose. But where does it mention chemical weapons, eh?"

"Isaiah!" the colonel bellowed. "Your country lies desolate, your cities are burned with fire."

"Fifteen, forty."

"Psalms!" Kyle roared. "On the wicked He will rain coals of fire and brimstone; a scorching wind shall be the portion of their cup."

"Game to Colonel Kyle," Ogden observed. "I'd chuck in that line of argument if I were you, old girl. The colonel's manners aren't up to much, but he seems to know his Old Testament."

The Vicar glanced nervously at his watch.

"He's taking his time. I wonder what's keeping Jere—I mean, Fergus."

"Maybe there was a queue," the Laird said hopefully.

He looked down beside him, and noticed the Vicar's walking-stick was leaning against an armchair. Whatever the reason for Beauchamp's delay, the Laird knew he would be back soon. And at that moment, the carnage would begin. But there was one small possibility, the Laird thought, as he gnawed his pipe. It wasn't much, but he had no other options. And the walking-stick was perfectly positioned: provided the Laird's timing was perfect, he could do it in one move . . .

"That sounds like Fergus now," he said, glancing at the window.

The colonel followed his gaze, and the Laird seized the opportunity. He swept up the walking-stick and knocked the pistol out of Colonel Kyle's hand. Before the colonel had a chance to react, the Laird cracked the stick across his face.

"Good man," Ogden shouted, and he reached down for the gun. But the colonel kicked away his hand, stepped on the gun, and grabbed the other end of the walking-stick before the Laird could land another blow.

"Fuck it," Ogden winced. "He's broken my finger!"

The colonel jerked hard on the walking-stick, and brought the Laird toppling towards him. With his free hand, the colonel grasped the Laird's throat and began to squeeze hard.

"Oh Lord," the Laird gasped.

The colonel was extremely powerful, and his fingers bit deep into the old man's neck. The Laird knew he was dying: the colonel's face began to swim and blacken before him, and his friends' cries were growing terribly faint.

Suddenly, the Laird remembered something. Many years before, he had acquired a black belt in one of the martial arts. Unfortunately, he had forgotten most of the techniques he had learned, but one ploy returned to his mind because he had described it in a recent instalment of Ogden's memoirs. It was quite a simple manoeuvre: if a man had his hand round your throat, you grabbed his wrist and twisted it, so that his elbow faced upwards. Then all you had to do was bring your other hand down onto the elbow in a swift chop, and the bone would shatter. At least, that was the theory . . .

The Laird gritted his teeth, and took hold of the colonel's wrist. It turned with surprising ease, and the Laird smashed the colonel's elbow with all his weight.

The colonel screamed and leaped back. The Laird hadn't broken the elbow—his strength was not what it once was—but the colonel was suffering from a nasty sprain, and the Laird was able to pick up the gun. He stepped back a few paces and sighed in relief.

"End of argument," he declared. "Lie down on the floor, Kyle."

"With your hands behind your head," the Vicar added.

"Fergus," Sybil declared, "you're marvellous!"

"Why, thank you, Sybil," the Laird said graciously. "It wasn't much. Just an old ju-jitsu stunt—"

"Fergus?" the colonel repeated. "You—?"

"Yes, me," the Laird chuckled. "Hard lines, old man."

The door bell rang, and Sybil rushed out to answer it.

"Are you all right, Clive?" the Vicar asked anxiously.

Ogden clutched his hand and nodded.

"I think so. He may not have broken anything, after all. Just a nasty knock."

He blew a nonchalant gum-bubble, and flexed his fingers reassuringly. Then Sybil returned with Beauchamp and a couple of policemen.

"It's all right," she said. "Jeremy saw us outside. That's your man, officer."

The policeman looked around them in astonishment.

"What the bloody hell's been happening?" one of them asked.

"Fergus overpowered him," Sybil said proudly. "Isn't he absolutely wonderful?"

Colonel Kyle was handcuffed and told to stand up. But he did not give up hope of a miracle rescue.

"Arise, O Lord!" he yelled. "Forget not the afflicted! Confront them, overthrow them! Deliver my life from the wicked by Thy sword!"

"Too late, old chap," the Vicar said.

The colonel did not agree.

"For the Lord will vindicate His people, and have compassion on His servants, when he sees that their power is gone."

"Don't bank on it," Ogden advised.

Colonel Kyle looked at the grinning policemen, and began to realise that Ogden had a point. He lowered his head mournfully, and recalled a more apposite line of scripture: "And the Philistines seized him and gouged out his eyes, and brought him down to Gaza."

"He thinks he's Samson," the Laird said.

"Well, it makes a change from Napoleon," Ogden laughed.

"Don't worry, colonel. I'm sure they'll find you a nice, clean cell."

"And you'll be in the one next door," said a familiar voice.

Ogden turned in surprise, and exclaimed: "Swinger!"

"The very same," Stringer nodded. "Only the name's Stringer, as you know full well, you stupid old fart."

"Delicate as ever," Ogden smiled. "Who are your friends, Slinger?"

He pointed to two men in suits who were standing behind the MI5 man.

"They're from the Special Branch," Stringer said. "I thought I'd come along and watch them do their job."

"You're too late," Beauchamp said. "These other policemen got here first."

Stringer glanced indifferently at Colonel Kyle.

"You mean this freak?"

"Yes. Colonel Kyle."

Stringer gave a surprised jolt.

"That's Kyle? Well, well."

"If you haven't come for him," asked the Laird, "what are you doing here?"

"You," Stringer said brightly. "I'm doing you here. Or, more precisely, these guys are doing you here."

"What on earth for?" the Vicar said.

"Impersonating Her Majesty's servants," Stringer said. "Interfering with the interception of telephone communications. And a whole string of related offences."

Ogden & Co. looked at each other in dismay.

"I thought that would wipe the grins off your ugly old faces," Stringer smirked. "You wouldn't believe how long I've been waiting for this moment. You just wouldn't believe it."

"This must be a mistake," the Laird said.

"A clerical cock-up," Beauchamp agreed.

"Are you sure about this, Springer old boy?" Ogden said.

"Oh quite sure, *old boy*," Stringer said firmly. "We've got the witnesses. We've got the van. We've got everything we need to give you miserable, smelly, incontinent old lepers fifteen years each. Merry Christmas!"

181

FORTY-THREE

The friends were kept in separate cells at the police station. Ogden spent two hours on his own. He had nothing to read and nothing to do except chew bubble-gum and wonder how the others were getting on. Finally, the cell door opened and a policeman stepped in.

"Your turn," he said briskly.

"Time for the third degree, what?" Ogden grinned.

The policeman smiled and took Ogden up to the interview room, where Stringer was waiting in a cloud of cigarette smoke. His ashtray was full, and the paper on his desk was blank, suggesting that the earlier interviews had not been particularly fruitful.

"Sorry about the delay," Stringer said, as Ogden took a chair. "But I decided to save you until last."

"Thought you might," Ogden nodded. "Keep 'em waiting, eh? Let 'em sweat it out. Good thinking, Stringer."

Stringer shook his head wearily.

"Look, Ogden. Get this straight: you are in deep shit. The deepest. So stop acting like a fourth-former, and start facing up to facts. You are going to go down, so you might as well do it quickly and gently."

"In other words, co-operate fully."

"You've got it," Stringer agreed.

"Just like my friends."

"No," Stringer said. "Not like them, as you know bloody well. They all refused to talk."

"Quite right too," Ogden chuckled.

"They all referred me to you," Stringer said. "I suppose that means you've planned it in advance."

"That's very observant of you," Ogden said. "I always thought you were a smart chap, Springer."

"Don't be a prick, Ogden," Stringer urged. "This boy-scout-code-of-honour bullshit won't get you anywhere. If you take my advice, you'll cut the crap and give me a full, detailed, written confession now."

"Confession of what?"

"I want your version of how you switched the tap on Blake's phone. I know Croft did the job, but I'd like to hear your account."

"I bet you would," Ogden laughed. "But tell me, Flinger old boy, aren't you supposed to offer me a lawyer before you start grilling me? I'm a bit hazy on the law, but I thought that was the done thing."

"It is," Stringer admitted. "And we will get you one. But I thought you'd prefer to talk to me first."

"Really?" Ogden blinked. "Why on earth should I do anything so stupid?"

"You'd be doing yourself a favour," Stringer replied. "Give me a full confession, followed by a guilty plea in court, and we can have a word with the judge. You'll get a lighter sentence, remission, and you'll probably serve your time in one of those nice, comfy open prisons. You'll have your own garden to grow spuds in, and they'll give you an easy job in the prison library. Doesn't sound too bad, does it?"

"Oh, heavenly," Ogden sighed. "And the alternative?"

"The full sentence," Stringer said, "to be served in the hardest, dampest, most overcrowded nick we can find. Fancy fifteen years' worth of slopping out your own shit every morning? Twenty-three hours a day in a sweaty little cell with three or four murderers and an armed robber? And one of them will probably be bent, Ogden, and he'll ram his dick up your shrivelled old arse every night. Fifteen years of it, Ogden—you wouldn't last fifteen minutes."

"Probably not," Ogden agreed.

"So give yourself a chance. Tell me everything I want to hear, and I promise I'll do what I can."

Ogden's reply consisted of a large magenta gum-bubble which burst inches away from Stringer's face. Stringer drummed his fingers impatiently on the desk.

"I'll only ask you once more," he said.

"Don't bother," Ogden advised. "It was jolly boring the first time."

"Now listen—"

"No," Ogden broke in, "*you* listen, Sprinkler. You've had your say, and pretty damned tedious it was too. Now it's my turn. If I were you, Slinger, I'd get the D-G in here pronto."

"The D-G?" Stringer repeated. "Are you off your head?"

"Not in the least."

"The D-G's a busy man, Ogden. He doesn't waste his time on rubbish like you."

"No?" Ogden said. "I bet he's been spending weeks of his time on me recently. And I've got something rather important to tell him."

"Sure you have."

"Please yourself," Ogden shrugged. "But I warn you: he's going to find out about this whatever happens. And it would be better for your sake if he found out from me."

"Are you making some kind of threat?"

"That's exactly what I'm doing," Ogden nodded, and with a mischievous grin, he added: "So stop acting like a fourth-former, Stinger, and start facing up to facts. You are going to be made to feel like a complete idiot, so you might as well do it quickly and gently."

For a second, Ogden thought he was going to be struck in the face. But Stringer remained calm, and said nothing for a while. Then he made up his mind and said, "All right. I'll get the D-G."

He left his desk and went over to the door. Before leaving, he turned round and leered nastily.

"I think I'm going to enjoy this."

"I rather doubt it," Ogden said.

Stringer left the room, and a policeman came in to keep watch on the detainee. About twenty minutes later, Stringer returned with an irritated D-G.

"What's this about, Ogden?" he demanded.

"He says it's rather important," Stringer sneered.

"It's about Colonel Kyle," Ogden said. "I know the whole story now, and if you don't drop all charges against me and my friends, everybody else will know the story as well."

The D-G said nothing. He glanced uneasily at Stringer, who seemed wholly unperturbed.

"So what's the story, then?" Stringer inquired.

"Kyle went mad, didn't he?" Ogden said. "It didn't happen

184

overnight, but nobody did anything about it until it was too late. The fellow decided he was some kind of religious prophet, with a mission to bring about the apocalypse. He knew the Iraqis had a chemical warfare project, and he decided to give them a helping hand. So he ordered the chemicals from Lemiers and used Carter as his insurance policy, in case anything went wrong.

"In fact, nothing did go wrong. The chemicals reached Iraq, and Carter was left helpless. Unfortunately, Kyle grew increasingly mad. It got so bad that even his CIA bosses knew something must be done. And when they found out about the chemical shipment, they ordered him to shut down his company, and took away his staff. They should also have put Kyle in a lunatic asylum, but they didn't. I suppose the fools just hoped he would quietly disappear.

"Kyle took it all rather badly. He thought he was going to be punished for shipping the chemicals, so he decided to destroy all the evidence, including everybody who knew about it. He murdered Carter, the investigator Hopkins, Lemiers, Captain Salvucci—and he tried to murder us.

"Now, what interests me is your role in this affair. When Blake tried to investigate his partner's death, all doors were suddenly closed on him. You put a tap on his phone, and silenced anybody who might help him. In fact, you found everybody who'd ever worked with Carter and told them to shut up.

"That's why you came to Jumbo Wagstaffe's funeral and ordered me and my friends to keep quiet, isn't it, Swinger? You weren't really worried about anyone writing their memoirs—you just didn't want us to speak to Blake. And I must say, Stinger, if you hadn't been so bloody rude about the whole thing, we'd probably have done as you asked. But that's all by the way.

"So, why did you take all these precautions? Because the CIA had been in touch with you and told you about Kyle. It was all terribly embarrassing, and if it got out, the stink would be appalling: the CIA selling chemical weapons to the Iraqis, and so on. Of course, it was just one rogue colonel, but try explaining that in the jolly old court of world opinion. And the British were implicated: it was Brigadier Symes who put Carter in touch with Kyle in the first place. So the best thing to do was batten down the hatches and pray to God that Kyle would vanish up his own arse. Meanwhile, the lunatic was murdering people all over the

185

shop. I'd say very few people come out of this affair with credit, wouldn't you?"

The D-G took a deep breath.

"And you're threatening to make this story public?" he said.

"Spot on," Ogden agreed. "Unless my friends and I are released immediately."

"What if we refuse?" the D-G said. "You're sealed off from the world now. You'll be tried *in camera*, and you'll be imprisoned in a maximum-security gaol. We'll take out an injunction to stop your lawyers from revealing anything you tell them. You'll be completely gagged."

Ogden shook his head sadly.

"I may be old, but I'm not senile. The story's out already. A few days ago, I sent a letter to a friend of mine in the United States. It contained an envelope which he was to give to a newspaper in the event of my imprisonment. That envelope contains the whole steamy tale."

"I see," said the D-G quietly. "It appears . . ."

"It appears I've got you over a barrel," Ogden laughed. 'Now why don't you accept defeat like a good chap, and let me go?"

"I'll tell you why," Stringer said.

He drew out a folded sheet of paper and dropped it on the desk in front of Ogden. Ogden did not need to open it: he knew precisely what it was.

"We aren't stupid either," Stringer grinned. "We intercepted that letter, steamed open the inner envelope, and took out your story. Bad luck."

The D-G almost fainted with relief.

"Well done, Geoff," he said. "For a moment there—"

"Piece of piss," Stringer said nonchalantly.

"I'm impressed, Flinger," Ogden nodded. "You must be smarter than you look. But that's not so surprising, is it?"

The D-G stood up.

"Well," he said, "if that's all we have to discuss—"

"No it isn't," Ogden said. "You surprised me there, Stinker, I'll admit that. But I've one more card to play. And I think you'll agree, it's the best of all."

Stringer sighed impatiently.

"Yeah, I bet."

186

"You see, the story's got out by another means. It's going to be published by the *Baltimore Bugle*, in my memoirs."

"The latest instalment?"

"That's right."

"Bollocks," Stringer said flatly. "We intercepted that fax transmission—it's a typical piece of made-up crap."

"It's typical," Ogden agreed, "but it isn't crap. Do you have it to hand, by any chance?"

Stringer nodded and took the copy out of his file. He first showed it to the D-G, to confirm that the instalment was no different from its predecessors.

"I see one or two familiar names there," the D-G said. "Carter, Lemiers, Kyle—but that's all it amounts to. This has no relevance to the present issue."

"But it has," Ogden insisted. "Let's take the last couple of paragraphs, for starters."

The concluding paragraphs were typical of Ogden's (or, more correctly, the Vicar's) authorial style. They read:

"I called London, and warned them that the Dutchman had been abducted. By nightfall I had fresh orders: Brunhilde must be bought off, and the chemical formula retrieved immediately—front-line troops were endangered. The CIA then furnished us with gold currency obtained from a special account in Zurich. Quite clearly, the Company needed Lemiers more urgently than Akhmatov's arms: they cabled from Denver, insisting that we make Brunhilde our top priority.

Of course, we didn't know that International Villainy, Inc. were guarding Lemiers with ten Magnum pistols, an anti-aircraft gun, and three tons of explosive. But I wasn't taking chances: Bertie Kyle gave me a Sten Gun, and Colonel Tompkins-Graham dropped by with a couple of grenades. (These had been illegally purchased from some black-market contacts in Iraq, but I did not propose to complain.) Finally, we located the Trieste safe-house, and shipped our armaments to a nearby position. Italian agents offered encouragement, but didn't have the nerve to participate. Not for nothing are wops reputed to be cowards!

Akhmatov's base now awaited us—with the vital, stolen chemical . . ."

"You'll know from my records," Ogden said, "that I was at Bletchley during the war. Learned a few codes, cipher techniques, and so on. Have you ever heard of the telephone trick?"

"No," said the D-G.

"You take a certain number of digits and group them to look like a phone number. Let's say the number's 01-894 7896. The 01 prefix is a red herring, to make it look like a genuine London number. The rest of the numbers are your code, and to decipher the message you start at the very last word, and work backwards. So the first word here is 'chemical'. Then you count back eight letters—that gives you the word 'base'. Go back another nine letters, and you have the word 'for'."

"I get the idea," Stringer said. "Where's all this leading?"

"If you go through those final paragraphs," Ogden said, "you'll get this."

He took Stringer's pencil, ringed all the appropriate letters, and wrote out the message: CHEMICAL BASE FOR NERVE AGENTS SHIPPED TO IRAQ ILLEGALLY BY COLONEL KYLE OF MAGNUM INC. OF DENVER ARMS COMPANY A CIA FRONT. BOUGHT BY DUTCHMAN "And if you proceed further, you'll add this:" CALLED LEMIERS LATER MURDERED IN COVER-UP ALSO INVOLVING BRITISH MI5. ALSO KILLED WERE BRITISH ARMS DEALER CARTER PRIVATE INVESTIGATOR HOPKINS AND ITALIAN CAPTAIN OF FLAVIO

"There's more," Ogden said, "but I think you've seen enough to get the point."

"And the newspaper knows about this code?" the D-G asked.

"That's right. We have the same kind of arrangement I established with Chester Peacock—you arrest me, and they'll publish the telephone code."

"Jesus Christ," Stringer groaned.

"I should warn you," Ogden added, "this isn't the only true story hidden in my memoirs. My friends and I know quite a number of dirty little anecdotes about the Intelligence world, going back forty years. Every instalment of the memoirs contains at least one such tale. If you send us down, the whole lot will come out."

Stringer and the D-G were lost for words. Ogden carefully

188

studied the expressions on their faces: he was looking forward to describing them to his friends later on.

"Mr Stompfweiner will be delighted to reveal the code," Ogden said gleefully. "Think of what a circulation-booster it will make! The whole world will re-read the memoirs, and—"

"I take your point, Ogden," the D-G said coldly. "It—it seems you've beaten us."

"Comprehensively," Ogden agreed. "In fact, I'd call it a first-class thrashing."

"Have we your assurance that you won't ever release this code?"

Ogden shook his head.

"Certainly not. Oh, I'll probably keep it to myself, if you people don't bother me again. And I also think you owe Carter's family some form of compensation for his death—"

"*What?*" Stringer said. "Now, don't push your luck, Ogden—"

"Don't push yours," Ogden retorted. "Now, if that's all, gentlemen, I think I'll be going home. With my friends, of course."

The D-G glanced at Stringer and shrugged.

"What can we do?" he said helplessly.

Stringer peered malevolently at Ogden, and said, "You're an old cunt, Ogden. You know that? An old cunt."

Ogden took the bubble-gum out of his mouth and dropped it in the ashtray. Then he smiled sweetly at Stringer.

"I'd take that as an insult if it came from anyone else," he said. "From you, Slinker, I take it as a huge compliment."

FORTY-FOUR

"More bubbly, anyone?" Ogden inquired.

"Yes, please," Beauchamp said.

"Encore," the Laird agreed.

Ogden filled their glasses with champagne, then raised his own.

"Who shall we toast this time?"

"The new Director-General," the Vicar suggested.

"All right," Ogden said. "To the new D-G, whoever he may be."

"To the new D-G," they said.

"Let's hope he fares better than the last one," Beauchamp added.

"How do you know the old one's been sacked?" Sybil asked.

The Vicar pointed at a newspaper on the table.

"According to *The Times*, he's just been offered a seat on the board of some merchant bank. It's not the most prestigious post in the world, but I expect it was the best the Government could get him at such short notice."

"We should sent him our commiserations," the Laird said, "and suggest he write his memoirs."

They all had a good laugh at this, and then Ogden said, "What about dear old Swinger? No directorship for him, I suspect."

"Maybe they'll keep him," Beauchamp said. "If the old D-G has taken full responsibility, Stringer might get away with a demotion."

"Not now," the Vicar grinned. "The book's put paid to that."

He picked up a copy of *The Ogden Papers*, which had just been published, and pointed to the dedication, which read: "To my old friend Geoff Stringer without whose kindness and encouragement this story might never have been told."

"Cruel," the Laird chuckled. "Too cruel."

"I almost feel sorry for the chap," Ogden said. "He tried so hard, didn't he?"

"Serves him right," the Vicar said firmly. "Football supporters deserve everything they get."

Ogden gazed deeply into an imaginary crystal ball.

"Mr Slinger," he intoned, "I see dark clouds on your horizon. You will meet a tall, bald stranger, and then you will go on a long journey . . . to the back of the dole queue."

"Speaking of long journeys," the Laird said, "Jeremy still hasn't told us why he went back to Holland to see Mrs Lemiers a second time."

"Yes," the Vicar agreed. "Why'd you do that, Jeremy? We'd written Lemiers off our list of suspects by then. What changed your mind?"

Beauchamp shifted uncomfortably.

"Er, nothing," he murmured.

"Nothing?" the Laird repeated. "In that case, why—?"

"I think I know," Ogden said, grinning evilly. "Jeremy has a new pal, don't you, Jeremy?"

"Yes," Beauchamp said hoarsely. "That sort of thing."

"Who'd have thought it?" the Vicar said. "Beauchamp, you old dog!"

"At your age," Sybil frowned. "I think it's pathetic."

"Oh really," Beauchamp complained. "Look, we're just friends, all right? She's a very nice lady, and, and—"

"Say no more," Ogden smirked. "Just be thankful that *she* won't have to visit *you* in some God-awful prison."

"Hear, hear," the Laird said. "That was a close-run thing."

"Closer than you realise," Ogden said.

"Not really," the Vicar said. "We always knew that the hidden stories would save our necks."

"True," Ogden nodded. "But it nearly went terribly wrong. Do you recall that I said I'd forgotten to do something in the States? Well, I finally remembered it when I was in that police cell. In all the fuss, I forgot to give Stompfweiner the telephone code."

The others stared at Ogden in horror.

"You . . . forgot . . ."

"'Fraid so," Ogden said. "And when Slinger produced that letter for Chester Peacock, we really were up the proverbial shit creek. It's a good thing the D-G didn't call my bluff, isn't it? I'm sure I'd have hated the taste of prison food."

191